A Novel

CLIF MILITELLO

Madfog
madfog.net

AuthorHouse™
1663 Liberty Drive
Bloomington, IN 47403
www.authorhouse.com
Phone: 1-800-839-8640

First published by AuthorHouse 5/5/2011

ISBN: 978-1-4567-5821-9 (e)
ISBN: 978-1-4567-5822-6 (hc)
ISBN: 978-1-4567-5823-3 (sc)

Library of Congress Control Number: 2011904882

Printed in the United States of America

This book is printed on acid-free paper.

TO MY DAUGHTER, KRISTINE

My brother,
Thomas

My parents,
Joseph and Lili

Chapter 1
The Letter

TaskForce HQ

Senior Agent Paul Peters throws a copy of a letter on Special Agent Joseph Sorelo's desk. "Listen up! This letter has just been received at our office and at news organizations all across the City."

Notice

September 17, 2011
And Every Year
Thereafter,
One Person
Will Be Taken
Out of Service ...
... to Remember
Those Whose
Loyalty and Service
were Dismissed.

THE LONE RIDER

Thomas Banner, his partner walks over to the desk, in the office that they share and picks up the paper, and says.
"What's so special about September 17, 2011?"

Peters continues the briefing "Two original letters were sent, one to Transit's ExecutiveCentr and the other to a Transit building by the Waterfront. As we speak, I have sent the originals to the lab, to see if we can lift any prints etc.

I want both of you to go and find out what this is all about and how we can stop this thing from occurring. Remember fellows, this one has got everybody, the Governor, the Mayor and the whole shooting match involved. I want this so called 'LONE RIDER' to be found and *stopped!* Whatever time you need on this one is pre-approved so, just get it done—BEFORE THE DEADLINE, if you please gentlemen."

Thomas says to Paul "Paul you know what I like about YOU?"
Paul ... "Yeah, Nothing!"
"Thomas says, "Right, again."

[Thomas has worked for Peters for almost ten years. Paul is much grayer now, than he was when Thomas was first assigned here. Paul has been the Senior Agent from the beginning. A been there, done that, kind of guy, but a real mechanic when it comes to doing the job. His kinky, close-cropped grey hair and thin appearance would seem to make him more suited to being a Math or Science teacher, than a Senior Agent. He's on a mission, to ensure that those under his stead have what it takes, to do their job.]

Thomas thinks to himself that he's not sure how much longer his wife Christine is going to put up with him missing meals and working late. Nothing like approaching your tenth wedding anniversary and having to say to your wife (and two sons Rick and Gary) that you might not be there to celebrate because you will be working late. How many times had he missed birthdays and holidays, weddings and funerals—even a couple of their anniversaries too?
It's a wonder that she even puts up with me at all.

"Come on you old married fart, lets take a trip over to Transit's ExecutiveCentr and see if we can't find out about September 17" Joseph says, as he puts on his coat.

[*What an interesting group of men, these three are. Paul has been widowed these last couple of years and spends most of his waking hours on the job. Joseph is recently divorced. Handsome, dark haired, a few years younger, high spirited and still in love with his ex-wife. He is now romantically involved with a beautiful Polish woman—and he never wants to stay late at the job. Thomas, is a prematurely graying around the temples, large framed, well-built man nearing the end of his 20 years of service, and will soon be eligible to retire. Of course, he tries never to think of that! Thomas and Joseph both like the air of formality that permeates the workforce here. For the most part, they always address each other and anyone else formally.*]

Transit ExecutiveCentr

An emergency Executive meeting had been pre-arranged this afternoon at Transit. Thomas and Joseph are there to meet with the Head of the organization and four of his staff. Thomas says "Sir, why do you think this letter was sent to your organization and can you give us a clue as to why the writer chose September 17, 2011?"

A Vice-Director starts the meeting, "Gentlemen, present today at this meeting are a number of senior staff, who can help you with whatever it is you need. They have all been briefed on the situation and why you are here." Everyone is at attention.

"My name is Matt Dorland. Unfortunately, the Head of this organization will not be able to meet with you at this time, as he has been called away on an urgent matter elsewhere. As to the date SEPTEMBER 17, 2011, it is *almost* a year to the day when the largest number of our employees *departed* from a single location.

Gentlemen, as we all know this agency in the past has put into place programs, that ask certain employees (those who within a set amount of time after arriving, were not promoted) to *volunteer for departure!* Those volunteers included, but were not limited to rebels, independent thinkers, non-conformists, and the like.Why, we were even able to get enough volunteers, so that we did away with having drivers for our top executives. We also had to lose a number of key people in order to be fair and balanced. *In fact, some of our best and brightest, also departed!*

While there had been other *departures*, including rank and file in the past, this was the most comprehensive. It appears that this very specific letter is making reference to one of the several opportunities/dates for those workers located near the Waterfront, to voluntarily *depart* the premises, as new *arrivals* appear.

9

By the way, as we want to fully cooperate with this investigation, you should know that those employees knew almost a year in advance that someday they might be asked to go. In fact, A large number of those identified, were given a second chance and were placed in other departments. Heck, some of them even wound up getting promotions. We hired a number of relationship experts to personally assist those individuals who might not be comfortable with their own or someone else's departure. Everything as far as we know was done legally and within the letter of the law."

Joseph stands up and says "OK, I think that gives us a start. We would like any paperwork associated with these volunteers, to be forwarded to our office. And, I would also remind you that this investigation is a serious matter and we will need to meet with your head of security, to go through their procedures and attach our protocols. We will also be taking several trips over to the building where these departures occurred, so if you can arrange for us to have access to certain VP's and administrative types in that list of departments affected, that would be a great help. Thank you."

In their car, fighting traffic on the way downtown from the ExecutiveCentr, Thomas says "I just hate it when you get all nice and polite. *Arrivals*, *Departures*—What the heck do they think they're running, *a freakin' airline!?*" Joseph laughs out loud.

"I mean, the information just sounded a little too neat and clean. *—It's almost as if the lambs, went to the slaughter willingly.*"

Thomas always seems to say what Joseph is thinking. "Besides who volunteers to leave a job? I'll bet some people there had a zillion or more years in. and then just like that, they were gone. I mean that would be really unnerving to anybody!" Thomas continues ...

"It just seems to me that if you read between the lines ... the truth is there!"

"Look Thomas, I do what it is I do, because I think that the more cooperation we get ... the more in the way of truth we may find. Besides. we've been partners for almost four years now and we have gotten our fair share of cases solved. I don't like that you rarely ever say anything in these meetings. I know you say you're too busy watching how they react to the inquiry. I mean, I agree with you that there's more here, than meets the eye. The question is, are we going to find that one guy or girl who knows the real ins and outs of the place. Someone that they overlooked or didn't take serious enough, who will give us the lead that trips up whomever we're chasing. I think my way just works."

"He or she may be one in the same Joseph, only time will tell."

They head to their car and take off for the Transit building.

CRASH!

They never saw it coming! All of a sudden a van runs a red light and plows right into them and spins the car around until it's facing the opposite direction. Thomas and Joseph get out of the car. Neither one of them have been hurt. They run over to the van and find that the driver has staggered out. He has a nasty gash on his forehead and blood is trickling down his face.

Thomas checks if he is OK. Joseph has gone back to the car to call in the accident.

"Are you OK man? You realize you ran a red light and this is just your lucky day because, we represent the law" Thomas says.

"Oh, and I'll need to see your license and registration."

Joseph meanwhile, fills in the details on his car two-way radio, as to where the accident took place and who was involved. And that they needed to send an ambulance and some uniform officers to the scene.

All of a sudden, the van driver takes off running as fast as he can. Two squad cars arrive on the scene and two officers pursue the driver on foot. Thomas hands one of the officers remaining on the scene a wallet, the driver had given to him. Thomas looks at it and says "You might need this, although I'm betting the info's fake."

Thomas and Joseph get back in their car, after wedging open the passenger door. The car is still drivable and they proceed back downtown. "Well that was just great. More paperwork to fill out, just what I needed. Guess it's going to be another late night back at the office."

"Don't worry man, I'll take care of it and that way you can go home to the wifie, Thomas."

They proceed in this car with a huge dent in it. Once downtown, by the Waterfront location, they get basically the same script they got back at the ExecutiveCentr. According to Security. everyone who left, did so ... willingly.

Transit building

Seems like no one was going to do or saying anything that hadn't been well rehearsed and approved.

They asked for a quick floor-by-floor tour of the building and were accompanied by some mid-level executives and a mid-level security dude, who never left them out of their sight, for a moment. After checking the basic security measures for the building, they proceeded with their investigation. Nothing seemed to out of the ordinary, except that there were so many empty desks on each floor. Why, there must have been about three times as many as those who were let go. Thomas inquired of the security guard ...

"Why is this?" The guard responded. "These desks also include others who retired or were not replaced over the years."

Since Thomas had been given a folder with a list of those who 'volunteered' on September 17th, 2010. He asked if they could see where each and everyone of them sat. He was told it was a fairly large number and that it would take a great deal of time. Thomas suggested that Joseph and he would split up and that way, they could cover twice as many areas.

Four hours later, they met up again and had pretty much done a quick bit of checking-out desks and drawers and such. They also checked the tightened security measures that they had suggested by the front entrances and rear exits in the building. These included additional mini-cameras that needed to be installed, additional personnel and a number of areas that were now roped-off.

Earlier today, when Joseph passed by one area near where a worker was let go, he heard a rather loud argument between two co-workers. One worker said that he was tired of covering for this other fellows' work and that he wouldn't do it anymore. The other fellow protested that it wasn't fair, because he was busy doing work his boss had given him, that the boss was supposed to do —*but never did*. Why, they almost came to blows over this. Luckily, a manager came over and quelled the situation. Joseph made a note of what transpired.

As Thomas and Joseph drove back to the office they discussed what occurred on September 17th. Apparently, not everyone left the building with their personal belongings ...

Parts of decorations, childrens photos, toys, tons of paperwork, books and disks of all types were left behind. And everyone of them seemed to tell a story. There certainly were some interesting characters at Transit. To Thomas it appeared that most of those who volunteered were not missed, as the place seemed to be running alright without any of them. Then Joseph mentioned the argument to Thomas and Thomas got really interested. "I may just want to pay a visit to those two tomorrow ..."

TaskForce HQ

Back at the office, there were a stack of papers dealing with this case. Transit had sent additional information and two junior officers were busy going through boxes of them. There also was a full binder left on each desk. This binder contained everything that could be found about the building by the Waterfront and everything that was mentioned in the newspapers. Seems that there was a lot of funny stuff that went on with that building. Plenty of stories about mismanagement and corruption that seemed to run rampant, involving this property. All of this stuff was compiled from the Internet and stories in print and from video's. Another big file contained stories of the men past and present, who have been Head of the organization.

And, there was a rather slim folder containing the report from the officers on the scene of the accident that they were in today. There was also accident report paperwork that was needed to be filled out.

"OK Buddy, I'll tackle the accident report and the folder on the building and you take the management stuff home and I'll see you back here in the morning Thomas."
Joseph set about looking at the rating sheet inside that rated every article by importance as far as Kimberly, the junior officer, could determine.

"I particularly like your sticky notes Kimberly, he said *This will blow your mind ...!* **Holy Sh--!** and *What a Joke ...*" Looks like you tagged almost everything in the folder."

[*Joseph was a transplant from the Florida office so, most of the stuff he was looking at in his folder originally appeared in the newspapers or on TV before he moved here.*]

He was amazed at what appeared to have happened with the building. Of course, in this Metropolis, he had to remind himself that people forgive and forget pretty quickly. Still, it's the Public's money. Multiple millions of dollars, no less!
How could they put up with such nonsense?
Also, it seemed like no one was ever held accountable for what went wrong at their building. Transit blamed the vendors and the

vendors blamed management and the press blamed everybody. Five minutes later, it was just yesterdays news ...

The more he dove into each of the articles, the more he thought he should be able to understand the culture of the place. The psychology, that's what fascinated him. If he could understand that, it could help him track down this LONE RIDER, like in that Mexican case six years ago. Wait a minute what suspect? there's no crime yet, therefore no suspect! Well, there's a threat and like Peters said when I first got here ... He took me aside, as if he was about to impart some incredible wisdom, and then he said ...

"A threat is the suspect.
The person acting on the threat—is the threat."

"Goodnight Kimberly, good job as usual and thanks Maury, goodnight. Man I've got to take a break. Think I'll take a look at that police report on the accident and finish the paperwork, and then dig back into that folder." Ok, let see what we got here. "Excuse me Joseph, on my way out I saw this report, seems like they caught that guy who hit you guys, here you go. Anyway, goodnight." "Thanks again Kimberly." he said.

No priors, no license, no registration, no ID, no insurance, no fingerprints on record. No KIDDING! I mean Nothing, Nada. Zilch. Amazing! The van was not reported stolen and ... they just let him go. Of course, he refused medical treatment. He just got a ticket for speeding and running the light, and for leaving the scene of an accident. Big deal, really!

Ok, this ought to be easy ... *Wait a minute.* What's this? When a tow truck attempted to tow the van, a panel in the back of the van opened up, and out pops a bag with a several Transit uniforms stuffed inside and shoes, ID's, keys and tools. *I'll need to know more about this*, he thought.

Meanwhile, Thomas is at home, soaking up the joy he gets from his two kids and that uneasy feeling he still gets from his wife. The fact that she caught him cheating three years ago with an old family friend that they knew for years, is still etched in her mind. Sure they patched things up for the kids and there's still love there. But every time he stays late or misses a family event, that old pain returns for Christine.

Back at the office there is a knock on the door ...

"Hey Joe, what ya got for me baby. I know you guys are working on this and that, you bloodhounds probably have come up with something."

"Hello Mr. Christopher Drake Sir, famous reporter from that rag ...The Daily Flush! And what brings you to our door? I was hoping you'd have something, you might want to share with me Christopher."

"As a matter of fact I do Joe ... Seems an anonymous Museum of the Transit donor has offered up:

TEN THOUSAND DOLLARS!

The reward money, shall be offered up for any information that leads authorities to a preventive action, by the authorities against—THE LONE RIDER.

It will be featured as the lead story tomorrow. My paper has decided to up the ante—*by matching the offer*.

TWENTY THOUSAND DOLLARS!
for any information that proves relevant in preventing this tragedy."

"Oh, that's just great! Now we're gonna have every idiot from here to China calling us with all sorts of crap. Thanks Christopher!"

"Hey wait a minute Joe, remember it was a situation similar to this one that eventually helped track down that killer at ..."

"We had that same information from just good old fashion, nose to the grindstone stuff ... Christopher!"

"Anyway, Give me another day or three and I just might have something for you. I got to sell papers today Joe, come on, give me a break."

"OK! Christopher, I got a hunch that if you get your sources on the street, on the trail of this guy that hit us earlier today, we might be on to something. As of now, that's all I got.

Back to work I go and next time bring coffee or chocolate or something to our offices will ya!"

After he leaves, Joseph starts to thinking. Man, makes me afraid to check my e-mail. probably at least a dozen bloggers snooping around too. I need to call my girl. Luckily, she won't be back in town until Wednesday and I'll surprise her with tickets to a big charity event that she wants to get involved with. Joseph, you are one lucky guy he thinks to himself, to have found a girl like Jersey.

He calls her Jersey, which is where he met her, 'cause he still can't pronounce her name!

"Hello Beautiful!, what ya wearin'? Lovely, wish I was there. How was the photoshoot? Work is work. Yeah, I'm still at the office, but I'll head over to Butley's for a drink or two and then head right home. Listen Jersey, I think there's a hockey game on tonight. Hey miss ya kid. Yeah, I'll water your plants and buy the garlic bread. OK, I'm tired too. Goodnight love." He hangs up.

"Long day, I'm gonna split in a bit, me thinks." He says out loud to no one, lets see what we got so far. We got the guy that hit us with all this Transit gear. we got a bunch of funny-stuff that went on in regards to that Transit building by the Waterfront. And, we got a couple of guys arguing at work. It's not much, but we got some time before the incident is suppose to occur. That's almost a year—that's plenty of time I guess. I wonder if the guys at the lab got any prints off that letter or can give any kind of clue about the paper or whatever.

TaskForce HQ

Early the next morning an announcement comes over the Intercom:

"Agents Banner and Sorelo
— I want you in my office right away."

Senior Agent Peters is shouting *"What the Hell is going on*? Our phone lines have been *ringing off the hook* this morning, with every crackpot within shouting distance, wanting to claim his piece of the reward in the paper ...

They seem to know way more than we do so far. So, what do we know so far?"

Thomas and Joseph say in unison "NOT MUCH, SIR!"

"That's the second car you guys have cracked up in the last six months" says Peters. Thomas says "Listen Paul, that first accident was months ago and we were chasing a suspect, and this one we were hit—it's wasn't our fault."

"Doesn't matter Thomas, I still have to listen to pencil pushers complain. Anyhow, I hear that you guys have a lead from that incident, so go find that driver and see what you can come up with. That's it fellas, now out of my office." Peters shows them the door.

"Hey Thomas, what did you dig up on that folder you took home ..."

"I ... I didn't ... I didn't get to it Joseph. I was having such a great time with the kids and all and then I spent some quality time with Christine ... Sorry."

"By the way, Peters told me they think they have a lead on the driver, I want to check something else out and after we meet for lunch, we can look at the driver info. Alright, you get crankin' on that file and we'll meet back at Bianca's Tavern for lunch and I'll fill you in on what I discovered in the building folder I have. I've also left you the accident folder with the report I submitted. See you later."

Thomas grabs a hot cup of coffee and starts to dig into the management history folder. Maury has left a checklist of names and amounts of time of those who have served as the Head of Transit. Thomas was pretty sure he had some idea about this organization. He was amazed at how little he really knew about all this stuff.

Seems as if some of the past Leaders were Marshals in the Military. It appears that they are appointed by whomever is Governor of the State at the time and they usually stay in their job until a new Governor is selected. There have been some interim ones and one in particular that stayed longer than most. The current Head has served for about five years. Some including him, have worked with the agency a few times before, in different capacities. As to its CouncilBoard, they also are appointed and some have served for rather long periods of time.

The organization holds agenda meetings on major issues that are confronting Transit and sometimes Heads of Transit have attended these. It appears that most of this is just a formality and the Directors carefully consider proposals in the areas of costs, openings and closings and the like—and then they do what they want to do because, legislatively they can.

Thomas' quick read on the subject leads him to believe that Transit is like no other in the State. Within reason and/or Federal and State law, it has been able in the past, to basically make-up the rules as it goes along, because it's an independent organization. And, although there have always been calls for oversight, only in the last couple of years has that occurred to some degree.

This report he's reading also makes reference to a third set of books that were found recently, and that, although the public and the usual Government officials are outraged—that particular furor has died down somewhat also.

"Yeah, that's my City, where everyone has short attention spans."
he says softly, but out loud.
"What did you say Thomas?" Kimberly asks him.
I said "So Maury, are you going to ask Kimberly out?" Maury
blushes and says "Excuse me." Kimberly jumps in with "Why I'd
love to go out with you."
"See how easy that was kid" Thomas looks at him with a huge grin.

Thomas goes back to reading the folder. It seems the press treats
all of these Heads and Council Directors like sacred cows and
then goes about squeezing them, at the very first opportunity. The
media even publishes status reports, based on how they think these
fellows are doing.

Based on what he's read so far, he feels that basically some of
these guys are way *underpaid!* I mean, why would anyone in their
right mind, take on a job that usually is unrewarding and frustrating
at best? On those rare occasions that something is actually done
right, someone or something finds a way to undermined what has
been done. Wow—what a place! Thomas thinks to himself.

Guess I'll take another trip to that Transit building and see if
I can speak with those two employees that were fighting.

Chapter 2
The Field

TaskForce HQ

Back at the office the next morning, as the phone rings.
Kimberly answers. "Thomas pick up, it's your wife on 2."

"Hi hon, what's up?" Thomas says.

Christine says to him "The school called and said that we have
to meet with the principal, because Gary was caught stealing from
the candy store, by one of his teachers." Kimberly answers and
says "Joseph you need to pick up line 3 now!"

"Don't worry, I'll be there." Thomas promises. "Yes, I know it's
important. YES!, I realize it's serious."

Joseph picks up the phone. "Special Agent Sorelo"

"Sir, I would er ... like to meet with er ... you about the threat."

"What threat is that?" Joseph asks?"

"You know, the one about the seventeenth!" the voice on the
other end says.

"Sure, why don't you come ... Ok, where do? ... sure I know
where Milt's is. I'll meet you in an hour." Joseph hangs up and
looks at the clock, it reads 8:45. Thomas is still on the phone.

"Listen Maury, if Thomas asks, tell him ... tell him that I went to
meet someone by the Ferry and that I should still make lunch.
Kimberly calls Drake and asks if anyone on the ground has
picked up any info on that driver and if there's any additional
information, make sure that Joseph knows about it."

"Kimberly, if I'm not back here by two, call Thomas and tell
him that I will be running late."

Milt's Bar & Grill

Joseph's unmarked sedan pulls up in front of Milt's Restaurant.

OK, guess I'll be on time, in spite of the traffic. The last time
I was here was for my brother-in-laws thirtieth birthday and that
was about 8 years ago. This guys suppose to be in the last booth.
Why am I always on time and everybody's always late, Joseph
thinks to himself?

Slowly, an elderly man, who he passed on his way in, walks
toward the bar, looks around and sits down on the same side of the

booth as Joseph. He appears to be a very nervous individual.

"I'm taking a big risk talking to you. You sure no one else came with you. I don't want anyone to know I was talking to you. my name is ... Nevermind! Just want to give you some information regarding this case. I want the reward money put in a big ... really big, artist portfolio case. I want small bills, not in sequence. I want ..."

"Hey hold a minute fella. You haven't given me anything that would justify you getting ten cents!"

"Oh, but I will. I'm going to give you the name of the fellow who put out the threat. But first, I'm going to tell you a little story."

This old fellow measures his words very carefully, leans in and then proceeds to tell his story.

"In agencies like Transit, you get all sorts of people, from all walks of life. Some are just looking to provide a paycheck for their families. Others just need a few more years to retire, and still others have no outside social life or family, and this job provides that to them. There are also those who are looking to have a career, with good benefits and salaries etc. And some just want to take advantage of the system, because they've learned how to work it. This story is about all of them."

He pauses and then says ...

"And then there are the *Buffs!*

Those who either, always were interested in Transit or they developed an interest, while on the job and it has become meshed into the very fabric of their lives."

He continues, still measuring his words very, very carefully, "Sometime in September—managers, waited in the large outdoor conference room, on the 50th floor. When an employee who was on the list of those who had 'volunteered' walked into the lobby, the employees name was announced over the public address system and they were pulled over, handcuffed and given the ...

"Walk of Shame!"

"What the heck is that?" Joseph asked.

"It was a glass walled area that others entering the building could view. Those other employees were asked to stop and watch these employees on the flat screen TV's in the main lobby. This was all being broadcast, on their very own internal Cable station! The selected candidates were escorted over to the elevators, where several armed members of security met them there. They rode together in the elevator and got off on the 50th floor and were met by several more heavily armed security personnel. They were all ushered into this gigantic outdoor conference room, patted down and given a scripted speech about what was happening to them.

"Redundancies! Waste! Fraud!" *was the gist!*

They were all told to remember, once you are wiped out of the computer system, you are considered a threat and are treated as such. Everyone was finger-printed and photographed and those items would be broadcast and displayed downstairs, just like mug shots. Pictures of them were to remain posted in the lobbies of *every* Transit property from now on, the same way as they might appear in your local department store, as if you were a *shoplifter!*

[*This wasn't how management had said it happened ...*]

Somehow, newspapers like the Daily Flush found out about this and flocked over to the location. TV Reporters and the like waited outside, to get reactions and comments. The reporters were hit with a wall of silence. No one wanted to talk about it, as they had all had to sign a legal 'Gag Order' right then and there that prohibited them from discussing anything about it in a public forum, for the next five years.

Can you imagine the indignity of it all, people who had worked there from just a few years to those who had up to 40 years or more, were all treated just about the same, no matter your title. Like they were ... were crimin ... *criminals!*—Imagine that!"

"Yeah OK, but I need to know more. I need to know who made the threat" Joseph said rather firmly.

"Well you know I'm not a man of means and I was ..."

"Oh so that's it ... you want me to give you some dough now?" Joseph said softly, with a hint of disgust. Still he couldn't help but feel sorry for this fellow who was dressed a bit shabbily and out of the times. He handed him a twenty dollar bill.

"Well this information I have, will help you solve ... well anyway, let me finish my story" he said to Joseph.

"You see sir, ordinary folks have mechanisms to help cope with these situations. There are families, friends and even co-workers who can comfort you. They will survive.

But if you do this to a person whose a Buff. Whose very life is consumed with certain part numbers and equipment locations and historical timeframes and such. There is no recovery! There is no redemption. There is no comfort that can be given ...

The awful shame, the hurt, the humiliation is just too much. The thought of being cut-off from their addiction, a lifetime ban from all properties and their pictures on display in the lobbies etc.

Actually, there were a number of others who could not cope. Well it's sad to say, but they either had *heart attacks*, *drank themselves to death*, or even were *driven mad* or *committed suicide!* Even they—found a mechanism to *escape*. But for the Buff, there is none!"

Joseph looks at him as if the answer is so obvious. "You mean to tell me that the fellow responsible for the threat was a Buff?"

The old man said "Not was. No, that's the thing—he still works for them! And, yes he's a *Buffs*, buff."

"I don't understand" said Joseph "You mean that this threat was made by someone who wasn't a 'volunteer'?"

"Why should he even care?"

"Don't you see, that's exactly why the threat was made. First there were others who were Buff's that were removed, so in his misguided way, he's trying to find a way to help them cope. He doesn't want them to die in disgrace, said the old man."

"And besides, just because he wasn't requested to volunteer now, doesn't mean he wont be asked to—in the future. Some independent thinkers were able to hide themselves really well, acted as if they were assimilated, but really weren't." he said.

"Some even bought promotions under the table. One day, even that will be reported in the papers, you'll see!"

The old man felt compelled to continue.

"Alright so, who is this guy and where can we find him?"

The old man looked up at him and said "Well, that's where I need your help. I don't know where he is right now."

"What? Are you telling you don't know where he is. Do you know who he is?"

"You have to go and find him, but I know who he is ... he's ... my ... bro ... brother! His name is ... Winston Allcus.

He has worked for Transit for thirty some years. He had gotten a promotion about six months ago and he's never taken a sick day, on the job, ever ...

See, that's just the thing. He called in sick on the seventeenth and I haven't seen him since. We ain't talked ... since, We haven't talked in days. I just know he's involved in this"

"What?" Joseph said holding his head in his hands.

"You just made me waste ..."

"No, you didn't waste your time ...

He ain't missed a day in thirty years." said the old man.

"And I should know, 'cause I've worked for them for almost as long and we talk every day. And we haven't talked in three days!"

"Christ man! It's only been a couple of days. Did you ever think he might just be sick ... so sick ... that he can't get to a phone or something." Joseph tried not to yell at the old man, but he was just so frustrated.

"No, you don't understand. There were times he went to work sick as a dog, with a very high fever. Why, he almost passed out a couple of times but ..."

"HE HAS NEVER MISSED A SICK DAY! EVER!"

The old man finished shouting at Joseph.

"Promise me you'll look for him, please."

"Look gramps, you think he's missing?

Go file a report at the precinct."

Joseph said as he got up to leave.

"Listen, I've got to go meet my partner. Thanks for the tip." and with that Joseph left the restaurant and got back in his car. If he hurried, he might make it back just in time for lunch.

Chapter 3
The Lead

Man, do you believe that guy? I hope I never get that old. Imagine wasting my time like that. Sometimes, I wonder why I ever got into this profession in the first place.

[*Joseph knows why he does it. It's because his father was a police officer who was shot in the line of duty. He didn't die right away, but lived in agony. He managed to hold on for almost two weeks before he succumbed to his injuries. He had suffered tremendously the entire time because as he turned to avoid being shot, he fell into the flames. It was a murder/arson case he stumbled upon. And it cost him his life.*

They gave an him inspectors funeral with all the trimmings, but Joseph lost his father. He was old enough to know that his life would never be the same because of this tragedy. It didn't matter that they called his father a hero. But that's why he became a law enforcement specialist.]

"Well what do you know I'm on time again." he says out loud to himself. It doesn't look like Thomas is here yet, think I'll go inside.

Bianca's tavern

If he's not there, I'll check in with the office ... No sign of Thomas there either, I'll bet ...

"Hi Kimberly, any messages and did Thomas call? Yeah, now he's gonna be late ... that's not like him. What? seventeen more leads were called in, since I left the office. Thanks Kimberly."

Maybe, Thomas got something good. Guess I'll just get a burger and a cherry cola. (It's the same thing he orders here, every time he comes to this place.) and just wait.

Transit

Thomas meanwhile has good reason to be late. He went to check out the two guys who were arguing back at the Transit building the other day. He interviewed one of the guys and he just seemed to have an issue with absolutely everyone. Didn't matter whether it was management or employee. He didn't even seem to care that a number of his co-workers were no longer there. He claimed that he did most of the work for the unit anyway. And then he preceeded to show me what he did and what the unit was responsible for, and dammed if he wasn't absolutely right!

Now the other guy, he just couldn't wait to have someone talk to him. Seems, he often found himself with a lot of time on his hands, because he was terribly underutilized. It wasn't his fault that management shifted him away from what he did best (years ago).

"The thing that gets me, is that they did that to me, so that they could take care of a couple of their cronies." matter of fact, he stated that "They did that all the time in this business. After all, his department was no better or worse than the rest of them."

"First off, in my opinion, they are afraid of some of these workers—so they leave them alone." He went on to explain that "these were employees that could not be intimidated!"

He seemed to come more alive with every revelation, "Because they are politically protected, some workers wound up in my department, as a favor to someone higher up on the food chain. Then, there are those who came into the department, had a bit of 'street smarts' and understood just how to work the system. They know exactly what they can get away with. They only steal just so many pencils, or they have someone else punch-in for them, etc. Thank goodness for the Union/Works guys, they're the only ones that really do stuff around here," he said.

"Others after coffee breaks, lunch and phone calls and hardly any direct supervision, work maybe an hour or two a day—at best. And when they instituted that Work/Home program, these guys probably wound up working an hour or two a week! You used to easily be able to tell who they were, because they always got a ton of overtime. Of course, they needed the overtime, because they *never* got their work done during regular hours. What a racket!"

He then looks a little remorseful.

"Look that's the picture that the press always points out and that the public has bought into, but there's more to the story then that. There are tons of people here who really work their buns off and never get rewarded or recognized. I mean look, if you're not a manager, you basically get overlooked. That's the way it is here.

Your raise, if there is one, is up to either negotiations or you're what they call a Capped employee (you didn't pass a State-wide test to get your job) The cost of living and everything else went up, but not my salary. Then, I have to worry about getting on that list that management keeps, of soon to be 'volunteers'.

And, how many people do they have here working double and triple titles. They were hired to do this and now they do something else, just so they can get a promotion and sort of bypass the system."

He went on to say "The other thing is that with my skills I could be making a lot more money on the outside ... I chose to stay here because of job security and because I'm really *proud* to be a Public servant. And so are a lot of my co-workers."

He seemed even more frustrated then angry, Thomas thought. I wonder if he has a clue as to who might be a suspect in the LONE RIDER case?

"So tell me, do you have any idea, who sent that letter?"

"Well, I think it was some kind of crazy, who needed a date or time that meant something to people and September 17, 2010 fit the bill perfectly. And look at what this *'nut'* gets. All this publicity and fear and heck, there's even a Reward! What more would some goofball want, then that? Sure I'd like to get the reward money, but as bad as some of these guys and gals here are ... **none of them are murders!** I'm sure it's someone on the outside.

As for losing my co-workers, now that was terrible. All the morale that was here, is absolutely gone. Now, we constantly live in fear that we might be next. Wow! And the people who were affected by the layoff's that had a couple of kids and big mortgages. Or, those who are responsible for supporting not only themselves, but maybe their parents or grandparents. Or, those with kids in college or parents who are were all set to retire. How are they going to survive?" *His voice now raising almost to full blown anger!*

"The thing is, that management doesn't really get it! They have no guilt. They still catch their train home on-time! I mean you give all of that loyalty to this place and that's how they look after you.

"No matter what happens, you're just a number. Yeah, I'm angry, he said!" *"I have to do overtime* and *they have to catch the train."*

"There are some managers who are always getting raises, two or three times a year or more, no matter what. *It's just not fair!* Of course, the way it works here is that if you give your managers a raise than you get a raise if you're upper management. So, of course, you're going to give out plenty. And most of them couldn't manage an empty paper bag. And for the most part they're never the ones who are asked to depart and they're the ones making the *most money*! HOW COME???"

"There are too many Chiefs and not enough Indians," he said. "I really wish that some federal agency would come in here (because of unfair labor practices) and investigate all these things that have gone wrong in here for decades ...

As a matter of fact, there's a guy I know. who really is the best kind of worker you could ever get and that he only got the bare minimum number of promotions in over a twenty five year career! Once 'they' put you in a 'box,'you pretty much stay in that box, no matter what.

And of course, there's all those unwritten rules that they choose to enforce when they want to, because they figure that the average worker doesn't have a clue. They just figure, if management says it's so, it must be a *rule* in the written record. I say question EVERYTHING! And if you go to the Internal Fair Practises guys or something, for the most part, they're really in managements pocket, so the deck is really stacked against you. They really stack the deck against you in here."

I JUST WISH THE PUBLIC WOULD SAY THAT'S ENOUGH! (But that's never going to happen!)

I remember, there was a guy who departed. The story he used to tell was that in the early part of his career, he showed up late one day to a very important meeting. The train he was riding in was almost two hours late getting into the station he needed. He said he told his boss that the train was late and his boss said that he had to go to the TrackRun Record department in Transit. They could verify, if he was telling the truth, that the train was in fact late. Well, they came back a couple of weeks later and said that the train was only some forty-five odd minutes late.

Management was all set to bring him up on charges and dismiss him. Anyhow, to make a long story short, somehow he got hold of some official Federal record from some other department, and it stated that indeed the train had been as late as he said. He was overjoyed that the record backed up his *telling the truth*. But what put the icing on the cake for him was that sometime shortly thereafter, one of the newspapers, probably the Daily Flush, ran a story that said that this unit that verified Track times, in fact lied!

They lied, so that the 'On-Time' average wouldn't look so bad, because of the way that the system was mismanaged at the time. **Yeah, he got a big promotion out of that one!"** He continues ...

"Anyhow, It kind of reminds me about that *'Watch Yourself'* campaign they have been running for years in the subways to warn you about safety concerns in and around the system. They're even in a couple of popular languages—*what a bunch of crap!* They don't really care about your safety. They just want to cut down on the lawsuits that they get every year. Your safety is the last thing that's on their minds, *not paying out lawsuits is.* And it seems that any monies that they do save, they wind up spending on Advisors and Design Consultants, to give the place *'a new coat of paint,'* rather then fix any real issues."

"Here's my card if you come up with anything else that can help solve the case. Remember, don't hesitate to give me a call. I'm Special Agent Banner."

Just one more thing he says. "It just came to me. You remember that movie about Vegas. I keep remembering what the character said in the movie.

'All they care about, is the dollars, Just the dollars.'

Transit is just like Las Vegas ... *everything* they do now is concerned with getting the dollars, by minimizing the cost of how they do business ... just like in Vegas, when they went from giving out quarters to giving out paper tickets. So, we went from doing tokens to the ClickCard. Same thing really," he goes on.

"In my opinion, they are just way bigger one-armed bandits.

They've been testing a system where they just reach into your pocket (I mean your credit card) and take the money automatically. They won't even have to make cards soon ... it's something they had referred to as a Clik&GoPass, that you can use on different forms of transportation. Only this time, it will be a part of your credit card. No tokens, no change, no bother, no ClickCard even. —just about invisible ...

—and just like *big brother*, they'll watch you too!"

"Listen, please don't mention anything I said to you, just keep it *off the record* or *I will lose my job!"*

Chapter 4
The 'Shakes'

Transit

"Oh, one last thing ... if you're looking for a suspect, check out Jimmy 'the Shakes' he's two or three floors down. Just ask around, everyone knows who he is. He the best horse-trader in Transit. If anybody has a reason for gettin' violent, nobody has a better reason them him."

Thomas thinks to himself, geez I hope Joseph has had better luck then I had. I'll check out this guy Jimmy when I get back after lunch and my visit to school, if nothing else develops.

He imagines Jimmy to be one of these tight-lipped, no-neck characters that you see on TV all the time.

Bianca's tavern

"Hey Joseph, what a day it's been so far." said Thomas with a bit of a smile.

Over lunch, they discussed their progress or lack thereof. The way that Thomas described what he had been through made Joseph crack-up on occasion. Thomas thought to himself that he was most grateful that he had a partner like him. Who else could take him away from the problems he was having at home, with his sense of humor. Who else would have picked up the slack or taken on the tougher parts of their assignments over the years. Who else would he have wanted to cover his back, when the going got tough. Of course, he could also be a pain-in-the-ass, when it came to splitting a check or filling out an expense account.

His reasons for doing things always made sense to him, even though they made no sense to anyone else. Why, who could forget the time he waded waste deep into mud to feel around by hand, for a weapon that the killer in the Bimpton case had discarded. Or, that time that he just had a hunch that Trivóre would come out of hiding and show up for a lecture on the matting habits of Sea Lions at the Zoo and that we were there to capture him, after all those years he had spent avoiding us, as a fugitive. Thomas smiled to himself and had found a way to deal with his partners peculiarities on somethings, for example ...

"I'll pick up the check Joseph, wifey has upped my allowance."

Which prompted Joseph to say "Well, I insist on picking up the check here the next time we go out to lunch." See, Thomas thought to himself, that's one problem solved. "So it's agreed that we'll proceed with whatever leads we have and meet up tonight, back at the office."

So, Thomas starts to head on over to the Transit location to interview Jimmy "the Shakes" Wilson. Joseph is going to try and locate Winston Allcus. Thomas calls the office to see if anything has happened in the meantime.

"Hello Kimberly, yeah listen, did that report come back from the lab yet? You haven't gotten it yet? Ok, what are the last four digits for the lab, I'll call them myself. What, it just came in now? Open up to the second page, near the bottom. And read what it says, please. Yeah. Yeah. OK., now look at the last page, anything about the paper or what it was printed on that's unusual? No huh? Well thanks a lot kid, great job. And my wife didn't ca ...

OH Shit! I've got to get over to the school first. I almost forgot."

School

He hurries over to the East Side and arrives late, but just in time to meet Christine downstairs outside of the Principals office. She looks beautiful, but is really angry. Thomas embraces her and they both sit down in the hall. Christine is on the brink of tears.

"You know it's your fault. He did this just for spite. After all, he knows what you do for a living. And, won't this just look great if he gets kicked out of school for this. Just so he can embarrass you."

"That's not the reason Christine and you know it. It's just things boys do when they're that age. Probably, he was just showing off or something for his friends. Remember, everybody told us that boys are troubl..." Thomas tried to make lite of it.

"That's not why and you know it—good thing he was caught. I mean who knows what this could lead up to ... Here he comes with his teacher now, lets go in."

Both of his boys have gotten in trouble before. Minor stuff like breaking a window with a ball by accident and a fist fight or two with some bullies. But this is different. The level of trouble is just going to escalate with Thomas hardly ever home, and with Christine being so tough. Thomas knows that what just happened at school means that things are going to get way worse at home, before they get any better.

After spending time with the teacher and principal, it was determined that Gary would be disciplined at home and would be required to go to detention for two weeks. He also has to stand in front of his classmates in school and tell them what he did. He then has to apologize to them and tell them that he has learned his lesson and that he will never do that again. Last, but not least, he has to go back to the candy store and apologize to them too.

After speaking with both his boys at school, he has to get back to work. And all this happening with his tenth wedding anniversary on Friday coming up, the timing just couldn't be any better.

Transit

Way after lunch, Joseph goes over to Transit, and meets up with Winston Allcus. They talk for a bit and Winston convinces Joseph that his brother was just over reacting, nothing more. "Look, I just got a promotion recently and I'm in good standing with my bosses—I've got no axe to grind with anybody."

Thomas arrives later, meanwhile he inquires about Jimmy and meets him in the hall on one of the floors. He is just coming back from delivering a package to one of the VP's offices.

"Hey Jimmy, mind if we have a few words, I'm Special Agent Thomas Banner and I want to ask you a few questions."

"Yeah, I heard you guys were around here again."

"Anyhow, anyone as unhappy as they say you are, makes you a potential suspect of sorts."

"I like your diplomacy Banner! Ever thought of being a doctor, you've got great bedside manner. And who says I'm unhappy?"

"Are you?" asks Thomas.

"Yeah, real unhappy. Pissed even. Unfortunately, I get to live. Come on lets take a walk outside"

Once outside, they go for a walk over to the park."Let 'em say what they want. This place is full of people that are privy to the latest news, and politics and everything else, but when it really counts, everyones come up empty. I mean if you want to know which employee is banging which married boss or if you want to know how they laid-off some people and then promoted certain people, at a time when everyone's broke. It's a joke Banner, it's just a shame really!"

Thomas listens to him and says "Yeah, sounds rough."

"I'm on lite-duty now and I guess I should be just grateful that I have a job. But you want to know why I'm so angry? Back when I was working on the train tracks late at night, with my best friend

Arthur Askins and a couple of other co-workers. *Something really terrible happened!* Anyhow a vendor had left a pile of stuff on the local track roadbed and we're real careful, just doing our work and doing everything that we were supposed to be doing. Like we had been doing for the last ten years or so ... I'll never forget that day, Wednesday, October 26, 1999. It was a little after lunch started."

ROARRRR! ...Thud!
"Then absolute silence, you could hear a pin drop."

He continues "Man it was so loud it sounded like thunder. Like the heavens had just opened up in the tunnel. The next thing we know is that we don't see Arthur man, nobody had noticed that he wasn't hangin' with us through lunch down there. He had just wondered off, probably trying to figure out his overtime pay 'cause he wanted to get that big pool for his kids. After the train passed we saw his body ...

"Nobody could have survived being hit by something moving as fast as that train was moving."

We were in shock. Nobody could believe that this had happened. And, to happen to Arthur. Jesus! He had eight kids, two wife's, one back home in Jamaica and one here. Six of those kids were his own. Two were adopted after his kid sister died violently, during a gang rape and murder. The man was a saint with a heart of gold. I used to go to his house for all the Holidays. So, after a through investigation by the authorities. Get a load of this. *The Advisors find that the accident was **his** fault!"* Jimmy says with disgust.

"That he must have been to blame. And, that he had drugs in his system! Arthur would never take an aspirin ... never mind drugs! Then, they brought up his work record and that he was out quite a bit. Man, sometimes he was, but if I had eight kids I would've been too! And, that he had been written up for insubordination twice. Those bosses were just assholes! Trying to look good for their bosses.

Man, it wasn't Arthur's fault!
But he wasn't here to defend himself, was he? So they put a stop to his monies and medical benefits and his widows were basically broke, because like everyone else, he was working check-to-check. Well, I started a fund to help pay for the families expenses and we

managed to raise some good dough, of course, it's *never* going to be enough. His kids are split up now, staying at different Aunts and Grandmothers. We also had to hire some lawyers to see to it that Arthur and his family get a fair shake. Nothing is settled yet, they're still waiting ... With the way Transit handles legal stuff Arthur's kids will have kids, before they see any dough.

Here you're guilty until proven less guilty. And if you are found innocent, they'll hit you with fines and penalties up the ying-yang. Everywhere else, you're innocent until proven guilty.

The vendors were not at fault. The WorkRules were not at fault. The driver of that train, that was going way to fast, wasn't at fault. The unsafe conditions we work under everyday. Nothing/no one was at fault, *but Arthur?"* Jimmy says, looking at Thomas.

"I DON'T THINK SO!"
Jimmy's look, was one of absolute disgust. The phone rings ...

"Excuse me Jimmy. Christopher, tell me ya got something. Yeah, his name is what, Ron ... Rimsum? he's staying up in a place near the river. Yeah, He's going to ... pick up a hot car by the park and try to get out of town ... Thanks again, but you still owe me."

[*It never ceases to amaze Thomas, how Drake is always able to come up with all of these great tips. Somebody's got to be feeding him stuff all the time. Most of the time they're even better than his own sources.*]

33

Chapter 5
The Gang

Transit

"Anyhow, you were saying Jimmy ...?"

"Wait, did you say Rimsum? Man, I grew up with a guy named Rimsum ... Ronald Rimsum? We used to play a little bball, he was better than me, but I beat him once in a one-on one game and it was the talk of the neighborhood. We were teenagers then. He's got to be around fifty or sixty-something by now, if it's the same guy. He was a real Transit Buff growing up."

"Did you say Buff—Jimmy?"

"Rimsum probably doesn't look any older than fifty." he said."Yeah, as a matter of fact when we used break into the yards to tag them, Ron was more into the equipment then doing his tag." Jimmy told Agent Banner that he remembered this stuff, like it was only yesterday.

"Alright Jimmy, thanks ... Here's my card. By the way, why do they call you 'Jimmy the Shakes'?"

"Well, I used to enjoy a little taste now and then. Never on the job. But pretty much anytime else. When I stopped cold-turkey, after the accident, I got a really bad case of the shakes. Some prick in the office called me that and it's been that way ever since. I mean the name just stuck—even after the shakes stopped, they still called me 'Jimmy the Shakes'."

TaskForce HQ

Thomas arrives back at the office and he starts going through his files. Joseph reminds him that he's going to be out of work for the next couple of days because, his girl is in town 'til the weekend. Both agents catch up with everything that they've done today and Joseph asks about how the school thing went down. Thomas says that it was painful, but his kid will not get expelled, just some detention and grounding. Thomas had forgotten that Joseph was going to be out, which is just going to make his fun job, even more fun.

"Maury thanks for updating my file with more stuff. Good work." Joseph says.

"By the way Thomas and I talked about it and it's just about time you two joined us out in the field. So, right after I come back from my little vacation, you and Kimberly will take turns with both of us, pending Senior Agent Peters OK. You can probably bribe him with a box of donuts." (A reference to the fact that prior to this job, he was a cop for years)"

"Kimberly, I see there are lots more calls, but no new leads. Do me a favor and check if my internet connection is still working and check my snailmail. Please give me a printout of all the emails and see if any trial date has been set for that Chinese kidnapping case."

Thomas asks her to also put away some files and to keep track of that backlog of Cold Cases, as some of them have been shifted around.

Joseph says goodnight and hands Thomas notes he has made on the Transit case so far. Thomas wishes him well. Thomas just hopes that things stay mellow while Joseph is away on vacation, unlike the last time, when three big cases broke all at once. And there was that chase scene, where he wound up getting shot in the leg. Anyhow, he has to concentrate on the work he has to do tonight.

Thomas didn't mention to Joseph that before he stopped working tonight, he was going to checkout that location where Rimsum is suppose to turn up. He stakes out the place and waits, but Rimsum never shows. So, Thomas goes home to his wife and kids. Joseph goes home to his gal Jersey.

[*Jersey's real name is Evasjalynski Ewasko. She is very Polish with a face and figure as good as anything in Hollywood. And, she really looks incredible for her age. Joseph first met her when she worked at the InfussionClub Cabaret, as their Marketing and Promotions Manager. She easily could have been one of their dancers. Joseph saw her, fell for her and got her out of the place as fast as possible. He gave her the nickname Jersey also 'cause he liked the way she pronounced that word—so damn cute, with that accent.*]

Thomas is back very bright and early the next morning, he feels refreshed and is ready to start his day. Wait, what's this!? he thinks ... because on his desk is an updated report on this fellow Rimsum and an address!

Think I'll take a ride over there and see if I can get ahold of this fella. "Kimberly, you want to take a ride with me? I know we said you couldn't go with us 'til we cleared it, but it's on the way to your school and besides it's just a routine visit. Oh! I didn't realize you were needed here for Peters. OK Maury, you're coming with me then, to the suspects location."

Rimsum House

On the way to there, Thomas tells Maury what's expected of him and that he should stay a safe distance away and not put himself in danger. Just go with his gut and remember his training. Thomas would go up to the door and see if anyone was home. Maury was to keep an eye out for him, but to stand back by the car and leave it running.

Thomas walks up to the door and knocks. He says "Special Agent Thomas Banner here, Open up, I just want to ask you a few questions."

He waits patiently and then knocks again. The door opens and there is Rimsum. Rimsum doesn't seem to want to cooperate. "He says that he has nothing to say and that the officer should talk to his lawyer." Thomas asks to come in and is told that, "that would not be possible."

The next thing you know Rimsum has pushed past Thomas, knocking him to the ground. He proceeds to run toward Maury with his gun blazing.

BAM! BAM! BAM!
Maury is hit and Rimsum runs past him toward the car!

Meanwhile hearing shots fired, Thomas rears back up and carefully aims at the suspect and fires a shot which shatters the car window. Rimsum had taken off, with Thomas unloading two more shots, in the vicinity of the moving vehicle. Thomas then runs over to see how Maury is and also pulls out his cell-phone to call for assistance. Maury is on the ground with a bullet in the neck. He is losing a lot of blood and starts to look ashen!

"Maury, keep this handkerchief on the wound and don't worry kid, help is on the way." Squad cars from all directions arrive and an ambulance whisks Maury away to the hospital.

Thomas fills in the Sargent on the scene and explains what happened. It all happened so quickly, and now an all-points-bulletin goes out for Thomas' car and the suspect. Thomas walks over to the house after being summoned by an officer.

Inside the house, three people lay dead (two men and a woman). They were killed execution style and in one of the rooms is a load of Transit stuff. Boxes with hundreds and hundreds of items from years past to the present. Hats, nice jackets, wind breakers, belt buckles, balloons, ClickCards, flying discs, placards—you name it, it's in here. Most of this stuff has to do with a Road/Ride event that Transit has put on for years within all the divisions. (Thomas remembers reading something about it, in one of the notes in the case folder).

Funny, there are no weapons, money or drugs in the house and no sign of breaking and entering, so they all must have known one another.

[*The two dead men, Mel Wright and Marley Davis, have rap sheets a mile long. Gunrunning, armed robbery and drug smuggling were just some of the highlights. The dead woman, Charyse Higgins, had no priors. Marley and Charyse were illegals from Jamaica. There is no known association between the three of them*]

Hospital

Thomas arrives at the Hospital, after having been given a ride by one of the officers. He is left in the waiting room, as they are operating on Maury, trying to save his life. Thomas waits until the surgeon comes out and says that it was touch and go for awhile, but that Maury is going to make it. Thomas sits and waits for his parents to arrive and he then explains to them what happened. He then hops into a cab and returns to his office.

TaskForce HQ

When Thomas gets back to headquarters, he knows what's going to happen. He is immediately summoned into Peters office and is chewed out but good. "How could you do it? What were you thinking? *Why, if my boss had his way you'd be in Siberia by now.*" Peters says. Thomas knows he is right! (And he's relieved that Maury's going to make it.)

"This City didn't need you stirring up another mess. Do you have any idea how many press conferences I'm going to have to be involved with? Do you have any idea what kind of paperwork this involves? ... Do you hav ... Aw, go on, get out of here."

Chapter 6
The Collector

TaskForce HQ

"I just heard about what happened to Maury. I hear it looks like he will pull through" Kimberly pulls him aside and whispers to him. "*I know no matter what happened, it wasn't your fault. I know that you were just doing the job and that this kind of thing ... I know you will be alright.* I have to go see him now, I left you some more information about the Road/Ride event thing on your desk. I'll let you know how he's doing later. Goodbye."

Thomas thought of letting Joseph know, but didn't want to ruin his time off, with his gal. Thomas took time and said a prayer for Maury, just a little insurance, towards his recovery. He also said a prayer for himself, he was in trouble and he knew he could always find comfort in his faith.

After all, that's how he had found his wife Christine. She was at a church social, she looked absolutely beautiful and had remained so, after these last ten years. Yeah, what was he going to get her for their anniversary? How does one make up for all the grief and anguish that he had put her through? How do you make up for not being there when it counted. Who would put up with that?

Thomas is lost in his thoughts, when he is handed a report. His car was found abandoned and torched a couple of blocks from the shooting. Blood was found on the upper part of the drivers seat. Well at least I hit him. Maybe, they'll find him soon. Rimsum couldn't have gone very far. Thomas puts down the report and opens the case folder that was on his desk,

As he reads it, he finds out that the Road/Ride event is more than a divisional thing, in fact it is an international event. Seems that winners from the events face off several times a year against others across the country and around the world. Attached is a story going back some ten plus years, it stated:

"*An incident allegedly occurred with one of the high-ranking people working the event. While the reason for the dismissal was not publicly known, one moment he was there and the next he was gone ... The story further states that purchases of 'tokens of appreciation' in the form of giveaways, were made to increase the morale and fellowship of the participants at these Road/Ride events. While this was a practice that had been going on for years, it is said that someone close to the story stated that certain quantities of these items were distributed based on a quid-pro-quo basis and that some of these items may or may not have been delivered, to those intended to receive them."*

It was stated that "A stockpile if you will, *might* exist."

Is it possible Thomas thought, that what he stumbled upon might be that stockpile? And if that were true, why would three people be dead and Maury in danger of dying because of it? On the surface it doesn't make sense, but I've got a gut feeling that somehow this guy Rimsum, this stockpile and that death threat for September 17, are linked together. If I can find Rimsum, I'm sure I can prevent this incident from occurring. I think he may be the *prime suspect.*

Still I'm not going to leave any stone unturned!

As he was going through the folders and reports, a random thought pops into Thomas' head. He remembered a buddy of his at the bar was into collecting ClickCards, since the day they were first offered. He had always thought that someday they would be valuable, a real collectors item. Then, lo and behold, later on they began to gain value. People are buying and selling them on the Internet and at trade shows etc. See the cards were printed in varying quantities based on who was sponsoring them or what promotional value/interest that they might have to riders.

So quantities were varied and the ones with the least amount printed or distributed in a localized area, were the really rare ones. I remember him saying that he was only missing two or three and he would have the complete set (and there were hundreds of cards). There was also a rumor that hidden among the millions of ClickCards that were printed, there was a commemorative one that had an unknown value and some extremely rare information and that it was printed on a very unique substrate (card material) called *Zinium*. This one-of-a-kind card has increased the value tremendously through the years. A value perhaps worth dying for? Maybe, just maybe he thought, that this stockpile of Transit stuff might be the reason that the shootout occurred?

The phone then rings on his desk.

Ring! RRRing!

It's his reporter friend. "So, I see you're in another fine mess Thomas. Well, I have some more good news for you ... One of my reliable street people told me that a fellow named Rimsum was dead. He was found to have two gunshots in the chest and a shot in the back of the shoulder and he had been beaten pretty badly, tortured you might even say."

"Shit!" said Thomas, as he reeled back from his desk.
"Thanks Christopher," he hangs up the phone

He was my prime suspect and now he's dead ... What if he was the one who wrote that letter? And tortured? What the hell was this guy involved in?

Chapter 7
The Fatigue

—*Fast forward now, to five months later ...*

TaskForce HQ

Nothing new has happened with the case. Transit has had some more 'departures' and a few more are scheduled. Maury eventually recovered and is on lite duty now, with a promotion. He and Kimberly have been dating steady ever since. Thomas survived the shooting incident, because of his great record and long list of accommodations. He managed to be home for his anniversary and bought Christine a beautiful ring and they cruised around the City that night and had a really nice romantic diner. He and Christine have survived their crisis. Joseph spent time with his girl that weekend, but they broke up and he has decided to stay unattached for awhile. Thomas and Joseph even managed to tie-up some loose ends on other cases and are working on some new ones, but none of them, out of the ordinary. Of course every now and then Peters will come into the room and ask for an update on the Transit case. Every couple of weeks he's told the same thing by one of them.
"We're still working on it."

Truth is that both agents have been bring in workers from Transit on an almost daily basis these last couple of months. Each one has an interesting tale to tell. Some are bitter, some see new opportunities, others are in rough shape financially and some are actually grateful! They are all told that they have been brought in, in regards to their investigation into the threat upon Transit.

Today, the Agents were introduced to Paul and Charlie Dorkins. They're brothers who work usually as outside vendors, They have a medium sized contract with Transit. They own a 'Fatigue' shop.
"What the heck is a Fatigue shop?" Joseph said that he had never heard of such a thing.
"It's a scientific instrument shop that rents out machines that check for stress levels in all sorts of metals and materiels. One of the ways Transit uses them, is to study and try to sound the alarm

if metal fatigue occurs in any of the equipment that the Public uses." Paul tells him.

They said they had a story to tell that might help us, it was somebody that they had worked with a couple of years ago at Transit.

"Yeah Paul what was his name again?" Charlie said

"Charlie don't you remember? His name was Lou Long, that guy was a real tall drink of water, maybe six feet six or seven. Probably spent his whole life ducking ... into doorways and train cars. Must have weighed almost three hundred pounds. I remember he said he was some kind of Ranger."

"Forest Ranger Paul? No! he was NY Rangers fan."

"No that's not quite right—he was a former Texas Ranger, as I recall."

"Definitely not the type of guy, to be caught sleeping at his desk. Yeah Paul, he was a real go-getter alright. He would constantly go get tea or go get cigars or a newspaper etc."

"Funny Charlie, Real funny. Anyway, he was a mid-level big muckity-muck, over at the Signs & Slogans department.

A real character he was. Why I remember his cubicle, it was full of all sorts of memorabilia, foam placards, statues and wind-up toys. Heck, you could hardly see the top of his desk. It was all stuff related to that animated mouse movie. What was the mouses' name Charlie?"

"I don't exactly remember the name, but I sure do recall that the mouse zipped around in a shiny red car Paul. Anyway, Lou was responsible for coming up with these "Ink Blot" people that were fabricated metal cut-outs that were placed at all the stations, and on all the equipment in the system. They had great big *'Watch Out!'* slogans on them, so people would avoid getting hurt.

"So, one day, we get a call that he wants us to run a test on one of these cut-outs to see how much the metal had fatigued over time. Why? Because someone had gotten hurt when one of them fell over and was suing Transit. Apparently it was his idea. It cost a small fortune to do the tests and he never told his superiors. He got into really big trouble when they got the bill and I hear that eventually he left Transit on some kind of medical leave. Apparently he was no longer 'sea-worthy', if you get my drift..."

"Sea-worthy—get my drift (Ha!) ... Oh! You are just too funny Charlie." Paul said that and smiled with a grin that went ear-to-ear.

I hear he holds a real grudge towards Transit. *He said that he was "seeking revenge by any means, legal or otherwise."*

"I think if anybody might be responsible for writing that note ... well, I'm just saying that you should go interview him, if you can find him—him being a former Texas Ranger and all." I think he lives over by some kind of beach resort that his Great Grandfather founded.

Joseph said that he would "Check the fellow out and see what he has to say."

Transit

Sometimes, Thomas and Joseph went back to Transit for the interviews. There was this one fellow that really told an interesting story about his rise and fall there. Seems this fellow, had been seriously considering leaving in the next year or so. He said that he had many people at Transit that let him know what decisions were being made in the organization and how they might affect him or someone he knew there. He said, he almost always had the 'scoop' as to what was going to happen, just about as soon as a decision was made there. Sometimes, he had it *BEFORE* other VP's in Transit found out about it ...

[*Since his job title was never a risk to anyone, a number of senior management people confided in him. They said that sixty percent of the information he received he could never share, but the rest of it was his to disseminate.*]

He said that his first major promotion in the job occurred when he applied for a job on *a piece of looseleaf paper and used a pencil!* He was amazed when he was actually called in for the interview because he could not believe that anyone would even consider such a reply. He was in no way Politically connected. Anyway he went on to say that although some other people had applied, he was given the job! No one could believe it. These were his words ...

"The guy in charge said that anyone who would send in what I did—must have the skills that were needed and that I must be hungry for success, which I was. He also proceed to tell me about the position, that I was nowhere near qualified for. He stated that he realized that, but that I had three months to learn everything I could about the work, because that's when the job would start. And, learn I did."

Many years later in my long career I was approached for a promotion. Seems it was between two other co-workers and myself, who were much better qualified then I. When asked who should be chosen, I proceeded to tell this new manager why the other candidates deserved the position, so much more than I did. They had the right education and experience like you could not believe. *Either one of them* should be the choice I said.

This manager turned to him and said "While it is true that you are less qualified, do not have the right education and certainly do not have the experience, you are my choice!"

I protested and said that "It was unfair and that he had to be '*Out of his mind*' to choose me." He said that a similar situation had happened to him once and it allowed him the opportunity to thrive in his career, and I should be grateful that he was an independent thinker. He then said "Yeah, it would be easy to pick the other candidates, but you'd be easier to work with and what you don't know you can learn. And learn I did."

Of course, his boss stayed at Transit too long and he changed and became a real company man. I'm pretty sure he would not have made the same choice, if it happened today!

Anyhow, as for myself, my financial situation will be tough. Losing my job is a challenge that I can probably survive, unlike some of the others who have left.

"I'm just going to let myself enjoy the opportunities I may find. Work for a new company or work more with charities or travel more, I guess. I made my peace with what happened on the job and have *a lot of people at Transit that I consider family and I will cherish my memories, and their love.*"

As he walked away, he then turned back and said to Thomas ...

"Transit has been good to me and my family and I've always be very grateful for that. I had a blast there man!"

Chapter 8
The Suspect

Transit

Thomas thought to himself, now this guy is definitely a suspect! He's much too happy ...!

I mean, everyone is somewhat angry, everyone is unsettled not knowing what the future will bring for their families. I'm told people are considering suing the place based on some kind of discrimination and this guy is putting out this story of ...

"Gee, everything is OK."

Something in my gut, says that this nice guy is really hiding something. I suggested that he should be available, if I have any further questions. He stated that he might need to relocate up north. I said to him that he might want to consider holding off on that move for the near future. He became quite indignant at that point and said *"What am I a suspect."*

I looked directly in his eyes, and after a long pause I said, "as a matter-of-fact—James Arrondi, you are."

He didn't say another word and quietly left the room.

Thomas went back to the headquarters.

TaskForce HQ

Joseph and I had gone through the list of all those who were released on September 3, 13 and 17, 2010. No one else seemed like they would turn out to be a suspect from those groups. We then decided that the best course of action next, was to check out any known 'persons of interest' that Transit had come across. We went through that list and didn't turn up anything unusual either.

We also worked closely with Transits' security department to go through their database of those who might have avoided paying the price of admission, against those with a criminal past. We also checked out all interior and exterior security cameras and Kimberly kept checking their websites and blogs etc.

And, remember that newspaper reward stuff? Well, as predicted, every goofball within earshot, came out of the damn woodwork.

We checked every one of those leads, and again nothing.

They even raised the reward to:
FIFTY THOUSAND DOLLARS!

Again, nothing of any substance turned up. Of course, the local authorities and Transit's security did a through job of following up, on any lead that came their way. They sent us daily updates on anything that they came across that seemed unusual.

The mayor's office and all those politicians kept in contact with Senior Agent Peters and he still payed us weekly visits to see what was up. Well, the truth is that there was nothing up ...

The case was dead as a doornail or *at least, we thought it was ...*

Chapter 9
The Reason

TaskForce HQ

Then one day, into the office walks this tall raven haired beauty who is then introduced to us as Miss Scanner Simmons. Seems Miss Simmons has some information to tell us that might help us unravel the Transit case.

"So, Miss Simmons I ... and before Thomas can finish ... She says ..."Call me Scanner."

"What kind of a name is Scanner" Joseph asks?

"That's not the name my parents gave me and if you buy me dinner and a drink , I'll tell you how I wound up with it. It's really pretty interesting. Anyway, I just felt it was my duty to let you know, what I discovered. I just couldn't keep all to myself."

Joseph says "Oh! so it's your duty? I guess you have no interest in the reward then?"

"Don't be ridicules. Of course, I want the reward and I always get what I want!"

"Always?" asks Joseph.

"Look, I'm not someone whose just looking to get by, I've always been well taken care of and that's how I met Winston. I mean Mr. Allcus." Joseph jumps to his feet and says "Wait a minute, we know that name. He works for Transit"

"Yeah, and he knows you know it too." She said with a look of defiance on her face. Joseph says "Yeah, I talked to his older brother. He seemed convinced that *his* brother was the one that wrote 'The Lone Rider' letter. He was sure that he was going to follow up on the threat. He was going to do it out of some misguided loyalty to his fellow Buffs in Transit."

Thomas chimed in "That's right. Something about Allcus being out sick and as it turns out, we checked it out and he was back on the job two weeks later. He had some sort of complications from a medical situation. Turns out he went to Mexico for some kind of procedure."

"He went to Mexico because of me!" she said it in a very flirtatious way.

"Why did he go for you?"

"Well, lets just say that he wasn't keeping up with his end of my bargain—*if you get my drift ...*"

[*Scanner Simmon's real first name is Krissy. She never knew who her parents were. She was a street hustler who caught that once in a lifetime break. A break by the name of Carole Sheets, a local madam, who seduced her and took pity on her, cleaned up her drug habit and set her up as her live-in lover. Unfortunately Sheets was killed by a jealous pimp, a couple of years later. Krissy got the name Scanner, because of her ability to Scan a room and find her next victim. Sheets had called her that and the name stuck.*]

Joseph had watched her ever since she came into the room. He was immensely attracted to her, there was no doubt. She was everything he liked in a woman. Brains, beauty and charm that had served her well. He just didn't trust her. Didn't believe that a word she said was true. Thomas liked her too, he could tell.

"So, how did you meet Mr Allcus, socially or at work?" began Thomas' line of questioning.

"Well, actually I met him through a friend of mine named Max Dorman. Max and him had a lot in common and they would go all over the country taking trips."

"So, did Max work for Transit?" Thomas asked.

"No, not exactly ... well, sort of." she said! She explained that "He worked as a consultant for a vendor that did work for Transit, from time to time."

"This Max fellow, how did you meet him?" Joseph asked

"Well he rented in my neighborhood and one time his company was invited to a fund raising event at the Museum of the Transit. I went as his date and we just started to see each other from time to time. Well, one day, he gets transfered out of town and he asks me to go. He really tried to persuade me, but I said No! Besides, I got tired of sitting home, while he went traipsing all over the country with Mr. Allcus, looking for collectible Transit items, they said. How boring is that? So since I said I wasn't going to go, he asked Mr. Allcus to look after me."

"So then you guys got together, is that right Scanner?"

"Sort of inevitable, and boy did he treat me grand. We went first class everywhere! He told me he had an older brother, but he never introduced me to him. And, he never told me exactly me what kind of work he did either."

"Alright, enough of the history Scanner, what else do you have to tell us." Thomas said in a sharp tone.

"I was staying over at Winstons' place, not much of a place, I was surprised when I first went over. Well, I was there for most of the day and he was supposed to be coming over soon, and then he called to say that he was running late. He said he wouldn't be back for a couple of hours. And, that's when I found it!

"Found what Scanner? What did you find?" Joseph said as he leaned over towards her.

She walked over to the window, her back was turned toward both of them. Then she blurted out, "I was just snooping around as girls do. When I opened his desk drawers, underneath some papers in one of them, I found three things that were very interesting. The first thing I found was a *number of envelopes* full of hundred dollar bills, there must have been ten grand in each envelope. Second, I found some kind of *report* about some concrete ordered for a job he was working on and attached to it was a copy of a note that warned that this concrete was substandard and that they were not going to approve it.

And then I saw it. Laying right underneath it was the *original draft* of that 'Lone Rider' letter, with edits written by hand, that needed to be made."

"So what did you do with the letter Scanner, where is it and what does it look like and what does it say? And where exactly does this guy live?" Thomas demanded the answers.

"Well, I was really afraid. Afraid that I was in danger. I put everything back as neatly as I could. Then, I very, very quickly locked the desk. Unfortunately, when I put back the key, I was so frightened *I dropped it!* I couldn't find it, no matter how hard I looked for it. I needed a little more time ... when all of a sudden, Mr. Allcus comes home from his trip ..."

She continued, still looking out of the window and then she suddenly turned around and said to them "I was all nervous and he was acting kind of strange and made me uncomfortable. He tried to make small talk with me ... and then all of a sudden he hit me, right across the face, hard enough to knock me down!"
SMACK!

Then Max turned and said to me "Where's the key?" (He had left it on a shelf, in plain sight.) He saw it was missing and he knew that I was the only one in the house, so I must have taken it. I was about to lie to him, but I didn't want to get hit again. So, through my tears I told him that "I was curious and that I was just about to open the desk, when he startled me and I dropped the key." He looked at me like he was going to kill me!

Suddenly, he changed back into the really sweet guy I knew. We had a great dinner and when we got home well, all I can say is ...

"The operation was a complete success!"

"And he's been sweet ever since. But I don't trust him. I keep expecting him to change back at any minute. I wanted to find that key and make a copy of that stuff I found in his desk, as a little insurance policy. So, one night I decided to use my charms and feed both of us liquor, so that we could have a great time in the old bedroom."

She continued with her story, more convincing than before. "Of course, I can hold my booze and eventually, he fell asleep. I thought now's my chance to see if I can find that key. I knew he hadn't found it either. As luck would have it, I did find the key that night, wedged up against the side of the desk, deep in the shadows. I opened the desk, took the papers out and snuck very quietly out of the apartment and down to the candy store copy machine."

The letter was a draft that sounded similar to the one that made all the papers about that LONE RIDER guy, but the letter didn't have that sign-off. It said it was from the *Buff Brigade* and the letter was two pages long.

"So did you bring the copy for us to see." Joseph asked in the nicest tone he had used, during the whole interview.

"No!" she replied. "I told you that was my insurance policy. It's in a safe place. I can take you to it Joseph, if you like."

Thomas look straight at her and said "Yeah, we both want to go see it."

"But I didn't invite, you did I?" she said.

"Look lady ..." Thomas was about to tell her that she had to comply.

"Now you look, I came here voluntarily and I get to pick and choose ... or I could *forget* where I put it" she said

Joseph chimed in, "Look I'll take a ride with her. She'll give you Winston's address and the one for her place. You will give him the addresses, won't you? Then, you ride over to the apartment and check out that desk and Mr. Allcus, OK?"

Joseph said it as if he was asking permission for it to be alright. Thomas realized that, that's what his partner wanted, because this way both things could be checked out ...

When they get in Joseph's car, she tells him the address and he figures it will take him about an hour and a half with traffic to get there. All this time she being really coy and sexy trying to seduce him in the car. Anything it seems, to get him from going to her little vacation place right away.

"So, does this guy know where this place is? Because you could be in real danger." he says with a real look of concern on his face.

"Don't worry about me, I definitely can take care of myself honey, I always do. And no. I never told him where the place was."

About halfway into the trip she reaches down between her legs wiggles around and removes her thong!

"Hey what the heck do you think your doing?" he said to her in a stern matter. She just swirls it around in her little finger.

"Look," I only wore those for you guys benefit. I usually don't wear any at all!"

She then sits back and puts her hand between her legs and starts to pleasure herself.

Now ... no matter how often ... he protests for her to stop, she continues. She starts to moan softly. Deep guttural sounds of building emotion. Luckily the windows are up, because the traffic is starting to slow down and how could he explain those sounds, coming from his official unmarked car.

As the feelings she is getting really starts to intensify, she starts to bring the window down. He puts it back up, she pushs the button to put it back down. By now her moaning is starting to really get to him (and every other person, stuck on the parkway next to him). She looks down, at the reaction he has had, in his pants and says with glee ... "Good, you ... (**Oh!**) really were ... (*My God!*) ... listening! *YEAH! that was just incredible!*"

Allcus apartment

Meanwhile, Thomas proceeds to the address he was given by Scanner and apparently has woken up Mr. Allcus. He introduces himself and then informs him that he is a possible suspect in an investigation and that he is about to ask him a series of questions, the most important of all is:

"Will you willingly open your desk and show me the content or will I have to get a search warrant in the morning?"

"No problem officer, I have nothing to hide. I'm more than willing to cooperate anytime with the Law."

He goes to the desk and then proceeds to open it and asks Thomas "If he would like to examine its content."

Thomas replies "Sure. of course I would." He suspected that the papers that she said she found there, were in fact, not going to be in the desk, where she said they'd be. As a matter of fact neither was the envelope with the money or the report. Thomas then said.

"I have some more questions that I wanted to ask you and would you be willing to come back to the office to make a statement?"

"No problem," said Winston. Thomas' thoughts now turned to his partner and he wondered if he was having any success, with his end of the investigation.

Scanner's place

Anyhow, Once they arrive at her place, he pulls her out of the car and says "Don't you ever pull a stunt like that again." Joseph's holding her wrist really tight now as she says to him "I bet you really want to spank me now. I would really, really L-O-V-E that."

"Get in the house and show me that stuff you have. Now!"

She enters the house and says "I want a drink first, that fun I had in the car really made me thirsty and what can I get for you? How about a *blowjob* and a Scotch and Soda? Your eyeballs must be ready to *touch* by now! Maybe a drink first? And in the meantime I'll go and change into something more comfortable. So, you want to see my *stuff* Joseph, I never thought you'd ask."

"Not now Scanner."

"I know, I know with you guys, *it's always business first ...*"

Joseph looks around. Not much of a place, it was alright cause it was hers and she had told him of her big plans to fix the place up, and make it into something really fine. This women had some big dreams and enough of a body and mind to go out and get what she wanted.

"Just give me the copy you made and I'll be on my way," Joseph said out loud, 'cause he's had as much of her hijinks as he can stand. (But damm, she so hot!) I've got to remember I'm on the job and if she really has the copy, then the case is well on its way to being solved.

"OK are you ready," She said, as one very bare arm shows from the bedroom door and then a bare leg. She has six inch heels on and a red folder held in her arm. "Is this what you wanted to see?"

As he stands up and walks toward the bedroom, she steps out completely naked with the finest, most toned and beautiful body he ever seen! He walks over to her, grabs her in his arms and passionately kisses her. She drops the folder and out flies a number of pieces of paper. As he's kissing her hard now, he maneuvers his eyes toward the floor and sure enough, it appears from a distance that she has a copy of everything she said she did. Of course, that will have to wait. as the passion between them has to be satisfied first.

Later that night, after multiple erotic adventures ... as they sit up in bed. She gets up out of bed and walks over to the folder, picks it up and places the papers neatly in it. and hands it over for him to examine. "See I told you I was telling you the truth and to think that you didn't trust me!"

"I never said that," he said, knowing she'd know he was lying.

"Look, I'm kicking your butt out of here, because you have to go to work and it's a long drive back, but I'd like to see you again, 'cause damn!" Scanner said it and meant it.

As he's getting dressed he says "Yeah, I think I'd like that too. He knows that he's fallen pretty hard for this one, because they seem to be cut from the same cloth."

She gets dressed, walks him over to the door They begin to kiss passionately one last time. She opens the door ...

BANG!   BANG!   BANG!BANG!BANG!

Five shots ring out!

Scanner has been hit by three of the slugs and now stands mortally wounded! Joseph falls to the ground, having been hit twice! Standing over the two of them is Winston Allcus' brother, Carlos. He aims his gun over the two slumped over bodies and wants to fire again, but the gun jams. He wipes it clean and puts it back into his jacket pocket. He then cold heartedly steps over the two of them and reaches down to pick up a red folder, gathers up the papers that fell out and steps over them again on his way out.

Joseph is powerless to stop him, as he was about to pass out from the loss of blood. The last thing he saw was Scanner playing with herself, as she lay dying. He said to her ...

"What ... the hell ... are you doing?"

"If I'm going to die, I might as well feel good about it!"

He'd promised himself that he would never forget her dying words.

It was a short-lived promise. She died, and he died moments after she did.

Carlos Allcus, the old man had shot them both and he was going to get away with it ...

[*He knew that Winston was protected and would be OK. He had shared a secret with his brother for many years. See, they had identical apartments. On the same floor, right next to each other, but no one knew. Since they did everything together, it was cheaper to buy two sets of the same furniture and since Winston was always on the road, he let his brother decorate. The apartment Winston had shared with Scanner on occasion, was actually his brothers apartment. That way, there was always one apartment that was kept clean and was suitable for entertaining. And if anyone went looking for those documents, they would be sent to the WRONG apartment and would not find anything in the desk.*

As to the reason why he shot the couple, he was madly in love with Scanner. Who wouldn't be? In his sick little mind, since he couldn't have her— it was alright if his brother did. (He even paid for the operation in Mexico City, for his brother.)]

To have someone else in her arms that was not his brother, (or him) well, that was just too much for the old man. No one would suspect the older brother, because *no one knew* that he had *followed* them out here. Somehow, he knew that she would wind up in her bed with him. He had even had Slinger plant a bug in Scanner's car and throughout both of his apartments, so he could listen in, anytime he liked. He loved listening. He used to listen to his brother and her make love in the apartment *all the time* ...

TaskForce HQ

The report came in and Thomas was called at home by Peters and told the dreadful news.

Thomas, along with the whole department, was in shock when those first reports came in. Two murders and the loss of his partner. *How was this possible?*

And why couldn't he have prevented it? He had no idea that things would get so out-of-hand. Afterall, she looked like trouble, but Joseph was no rookie, he knew how to handle himself.

Still, there was no sign of a break-in, so it must have been someone she knew.

Yet, the report from the crime scene stated that it looked like the murders might have been done by a professional. Everything had been wiped clean. No fingerprints, no shell casings, no footprints, no tire tracks—nothing at all out of place.

Of course the papers, had a field day with the story. There were several different headlines in The Daily Flush that week."

THE DAILY FLUSH

**RAVEN HAIRED BEAUTY FOUND MURDERED
ALONG WITH A HIGH PROFILE INVESTIGATOR**
and
**SOFT SPOT FOR LOVER LEADS TO
TWO MURDERS**
and of course
**ACTRESS FAMOUS IN DEATH LIKE
SHE NEVER WAS IN LIFE.**

Those guys will do anything to sell papers. She was no actress, but maybe she did just play. the best role of her life ...

Thomas had already been up to the cabin, to have a look around the morning after the murders, so he concurred with the reports he had read. And of course, no copy of the report she said she had copied was found. He carefully looked through the notes that Joseph had kept and checked his cell-phone. And he had even gotten over to his partners apartment to see if he had any notes or if he could find any clues. Nothing seemed to stand out.

Thomas' office was inundated with reporters trying to get any leads they could. Of course, they kept these guys away from Thomas as much as they could. Even Drake, the reporter wasn't getting through to him. Still, stories were written, even by Drake.

These stories went into the fact that she had been found dead just inside the door and that the Agent was found nearby. There was evidence that they had been lovers and that he went with her to follow up on a lead. It went on to say that they had been shot by a 45 caliber revolver, and that the gun was not found at the scene or in the immediate surroundings. And of course, his partner Thomas Banner's name had also made its way into the papers and that caused nothing, but grief for Thomas.

Since Joseph's biggest profile case was the *"Murder at Transit"* case as they called it. This must have had something to do with it. They also put together the string of murders that had happened in the last couple of months and tied them altogether into a nice neat bow. They questioned how good a job had these partners done, as they were no closer to solving that case or this one, for that matter.

The public loves a mystery and waited with baited breath for every little tidbit they could get their hands on, in the morning papers.

The stories would run for a full two week in the Daily Flush.

Didn't matter that Christopher Drake was considered a friend and drinking buddy. He still had to do his job and *sell papers!*

The fact that Thomas came to work everyday through all of this was kind of strange. But it was the only way to keep himself sane and focused. Agent Peters had suggested that he take a little time away from the job, so that he might come back fresh. It was even suggested that he take use a little vacation time. He refused.

[*Now promoted posthumously to Senior Agent Joseph Sorelo, he was given an Inspectors funeral along with all the pomp and circumstance. The funeral was televised and some two thousand uniformed and plainclothes officers were in attendance. The general public flocked to the Mass and funeral home in large numbers. A real circus between the press and the TV and Cable reporters occurred. Today he was eulogized, tomorrow, Joseph would be **forgotten** .... by those he had served.*]

Thomas had really wanted absolutely no part in the services. But for the sake of his partners' honor and for the department itself—he participated. He really did not want his grief to be on public display. He had lost a comrade, a partner, a brother, a friend.

Of course all of this anger, frustration and grief had taken a toll on his marriage. He moved out, (at his wife's suggestion), so that they might be able to salvage their marriage later. She felt that they needed the time and if and when he was ready, he might be able to come back. After all, it wasn't fair to his boys and he knew it. He actually moved into his partners apartment temporarily.

Joseph's apartment

The landlord said it would be alright for him to stay, until the end of the month, since the rent was payed for and he knew that Joseph had been his partner.

Once he moved in there, He wanted time to grieve. He found himself talking to his dead partner. Asking Joseph to help him, solve the murders. He felt that maybe, if he stayed at the apartment, he might be able to get some insight, as to what happened. Maybe if would help him stay sane (or drive him deeper into madness!).

Well, the end of the month was rapidly approaching now and Thomas and the department were no closer to solving the murders. Thomas was starting to come unhinged. Of course, talking to Jersey helped ease the pain. They could comfort one another.

Thomas also found as much time as he could, to spend with his sons as was possible, from then on. When he wasn't with them or the wife, he could usually be found at the neighboring watering hole. Maybe if I get drunk enough, often enough, it will dull the pain. It was a wonder how he managed to still go to work and do his job. He was more determined then ever to pursue any lead that might help him, no matter how small. He needed something.

Bianca's

Then, one night, Gail Diaz found him at the bar. She said "I'm sorry to bother you, but I wanted to tell you something that might help you solve the case of The Lone Rider."
Thomas looked at her, finished his drink and said ...
"Why now, why here and how do you know who I am!?"

She said "Well, you have been on TV quite a bit and I asked around, and someone said that this is where you could be found most nights. As to why now, I wasn't sure if I should get involved with this whole thing. I don't really want to put myself in jeopardy. After all this situation in very serious indeed."
"And why would you be doing that?" Thomas asked

"Can we go over to that booth and talk?" Gail asked

"Oh! and would you like a drink—no, on second thought, I don't think you're going to are you? Please tell what's on your mind kid." said Thomas, in a most cynically unpleasing voice.

"I've worked for Transit some 22 years and have risen to the title of Prime Secretary to one of the VP's. I have served in that capacity for these past four years. Most of the time, it concerns general office work and confidential correspondence. Usually most of these internal letters concern directives moving Transit foward, towards reorganizing it's structure. They sometimes also deal with finding ways to reach strategic objectives and/or in placing cost-saving measures, in place. In this position, I have come across items or been privy to conversations from time to time that on the surface could be or are morally, or esthetically suspect."

"So you got a case of wanting to unburden your conscience kid?" Thomas says, quite disrespectful way.

"No, that's not it at all. I'm just trying to help you with your investigation, but if you *don't want to hear what I have to say* then, I can just leave now, if you like. And by the way I'm not a kid and I resent you calling me that, my name is Gail Diaz!"

Thomas realizes that he's been acting like a jerk and apologizes to her and says "Please continue."

"Anyway this one day I overhear the tail end of a conversation my boss was having. She has been under a lot of pressure lately and was very upset on the phone." She then took a long pause, as I walked in and said "I'm not going to do your dirty work any longer!" she hung up the phone so hard, the handset cracked.

"Beatty Morgenstern, my boss, then directed me to pull all of the files, on this huge purchase of computer equipment done many years ago and then she slammed the door. She spent all day reviewing the files and did not want to be disturbed and near the end of the day, she asked if I could stay a little later. Now, as a rule, she never missed that 5:08 train, so this was indeed a strange request." I surmised that something really disturbing was going on.

"When I went into her room, it appeared she had been sobbing. She continued crying for a minute or two and then got her composure back." I said to her "Beatty what has you so upset and how can I help? Are you and your family alright?" Beatty looked at me and said "I have no one to turn to and I need you to swear to me that you will not tell a soul." Gail said "It would be our secret."

"I afraid, *I'm deathly afraid!*" Beatty said as tears weld up in her eyes again. "I'm deathly afraid because, I just got a note from ...

THE LONE RIDER. I really believe that he is going to *target me.* that I'm going to be **killed!**"

Gail was stunned at what she was hearing. "And what makes you so sure that you are going to be the target and besides there's tons of security here, and you can certainly afford to hire some outside personnel, if need be."

Beatty looked at Gail and said matter-of-factly

"You don't understand, if someone wants to kill you—then they are going to kill you. It's just that simple and I really love my kids and my husband and I am afraid."

Don't worry I said "There are people investigating that threat by the Lone Rider and they'll catch whoever is responsible before anything bad happens."

"It's been months and months and they haven't caught anyone, and it's getting closer and closer to the deadline ..." Beatty said.

She then continued and said "Years ago I was, responsible for ordering millions of dollars of computer equipment that I knew was surely inferior, and worse then that, it would give an 'in' to a company that was very *ruthless* in their business approach. This company put in some proprietary hardware and software that could not easily (or ever) be replaced. They knew that the equipment that they sold us was going to fail, in the very short term. And, if we took steps to have this vendor replaced, that we would not be able to function without calling them back as consultants. They would then sit back and bleed us dry. Not a position that we would want to find ourselves in at all ...

And that's exactly what happened. The thing is, I was ordered to buy this equipment and my guess is that it came all the way from the top. And, I am going to be the *scapegoat* that Transit uses. I am going to be blamed for the unbelieveable financial disaster that they are in NOW!

So you see, it wasn't fiscal irresponsibility or mismanagement by Transit in general. Nor was it the Cities fiscal crisis. *Ultimately, I am the one that has been responsible for those who have been let go at Transit!* And whoever put out that threat knows or has figured out, that I'm RESPONSIBLE. *I'm the logical target!*

"*But that's crazy!* no one could have figured that out. I just found that out and I've worked closely with you for the last 4 years and had no clue." Gail said, trying her best to reassure her.

"As for these departures at Transit. It didn't fall under your jurisdiction. Tons of departments were involved. OK, yeah, our department took a lot of hits, but we had more personnel than we needed ... right?" Gail was sure this would console her, but it really did not. Beatty was in a state of almost shear panic.

"GAIL, IT BEEN ALL A COVER UP!"
—She continued "Don't you see?" Beatty tried to explain ...

"We bought all this *bad equipment*, then we hired all of this extra personnel to gear up and then we were left with this glut of people in EVERY department, Didn't you ever notice that in this building, after all of us moved in, there were still tons of empty cubicles and offices. That was in anticipation of Transit having to hire even more people. It was all because of this decision. Meanwhile, Transit has just been hemorrhaging money from expenses and salaries and the leasing of space here and at a lot of Transit properties elsewhere."

She continued "We went out and had to buy another, even more expensive set of hardware and software to replace all this stuff that was junk. Every department then had to help us hide all of the actual dollars we were spending. Sort of, spread the burden around on paper, so that the Feds and others wouldn't get wise to what we were doing. This was going to be a monumental task. So, again we needed to hire even more personnel. We then started counting employees twice, even three times each, again on paper."

Beatty then said "Of course, we hired some of the best people in the place, to think of ways for us to '*fudge*' the books even more. From the Advertising department to those in the trenches, every department was ordered to pitch in!"

"So, lets say they printed a really large quantity of brochures and posters—they recorded that they printed twice or ten times as much. And, *nobody ever checked our methods*. Not the Feds, not the State, not the City—just amazing! Cleaners used four or five times the numbers of cleaning solutions as they normally would. Of course, there's a zillion other examples I could give you. Now, the bean counters can't even keep track anymore of the ways in which they lied. Why? In typical Transit fashion, some of those bean counters were told to *depart*—and they were the ones who had come up with the original 'fudge-factor' numbers in the first place! Now, nobody knows what's real and what's not ...

Luckily, at the time, there really wasn't any oversight of any kind on what we had been doing." Beatty was just beside herself now. "Again the money we spent, remember a huge part of it, had come from the Feds, well they started to make some inquiries. For example: They asked, why we followed certain practises:

'Allegedly', One source—(huge) contracts awarded time and again, to the *same* exact vendors. Possible Bid riggings etc.? The perception that Minority vendors were excluded in the process!

Not to mention, Drake and other investigative reporters, filing exposés almost daily! The pressure was enormous ..."

She's is really drained now. "It just seemed to get deeper and deeper—*a vicious merry-go-round cycle that I couldn't get off!*

The next thing you know, questions are being asked and talk of a U.S. Government 'Oversight Committee' being formed to investigate us. So, in order to nip that one in the bud and because the heat had really been turned up, and Transit was in the spotlight. Those in power here figured that they would *voluntarily* call for creating their own oversight and promised to do a lot more audits—both internal and external." She continued ...

"Nothing like the 'fox guarding the hen-house'!" She said.

"And of course, we had our share of *Whistleblowers* too! We dealt effectively with most, by 'painting' them in *newspapers that cater to us*, as very 'Disgruntled, Self-Serving current or former employees."

And another thing. "Why do you think most of the technical advances in Transit, *never* turn out the way *we* say they will?!"

"Think about it?" she said. "If that equipment really worked, then we'd have to account for the money in real dollars, without any cost overruns! Why do you think every thing we attempt to do is called a (TTP) Test/Trial Pilot. Because, as soon as it's given that name, then internally that's a clue that we intend to dump cost overruns onto it. If the public gets upset about stuff not working, *we can always blame the vendors!* That way are hands are always clean to the Public. If it turns out that one of the TTP's is successful, we deal with that, by hiring someone dreadful, to maintain it. Or better still, we take over the maintenance and then have a field day with burying costs. Sometimes we even buy stuff that works, you know—mix-it up a bit—just so no one catches on to what we are doing. Heck, we've even taken to doing some jobs in-house—if a vendor won't work with us to increase the costs enough. Then we can ensure that the costs skyrocket, on paper."

"Take that ClickCard and all the technology that goes with it. The final decision was between three or four companies and in the final analysis, which two do you think were chosen, That's right. The ones with vendors that clearly faced more challenges then the others, but who would work with us—*If you know what I mean.*

Later, those two companies even provided places to work, for certain Big-Whigs, after their careers at Transit were over. I was even offered a position at one point." Beatty said.

Wait a minute. Gail said "Getting back to your reason for being afraid of the LONE RIDER—didn't you ever consider that it might just be *some kind of a nut,* that's not bright enough to figure all this out?"

"Yes, I did, but as far as I know, I was the only individual in Transit who received an original note. (*And it was addressed to me personally.*)"

"Here!" Beatty said "Go ahead and read it and especially the postscript at the bottom!" Gail looked at the letter carefully and could not believe what it said at the bottom of it:

"REMEMBER BEATTY, I KNOW WHAT YOU KNOW AND MORE ... THE LONE RIDER." *It took her breath away!*

"You know, I *NEVER* showed that letter to the authorities." There was a look on Beatty's face, almost of regret. "How could I? Then I would have to tell them everything that I've just told you. Pretty soon I'd be out of a job and would make a much easier target. So you see, you are the only one I trust Gail." She walked over and grabbed Gail's hand.

"Why don't you go to the authorities and tell them that you have this letter. I'm sure they'd be able to protect you. I mean, if you don't tell someone like the police an such, then you have absolutely no protection at all. And, if you are right, then you are a sitting duck!" Gail said it and then realized that she now knows what Beatty knows. *And, whose going to protect her?*

Beatty then told her that she already felt better, now that she had shared the burden of her situation with someone. They said goodnight and Beatty again asked Gail to swear that she wouldn't tell a soul and that they should speak again on Monday.

"When I left Beatty's office, I realized that I had no choice, but to go to the authorities. I really could not have walked out on you. I needed you." Gail said, sounding so desperate that Thomas was convinced, she was telling the truth.

"Look Gail, I can lie and tell you everything is going to be alright, but the department hasn't come up with anything in quite awhile and the deadline is still looming." Thomas tried to be as honest and forthcoming, as he possibly could be.

"Gail, you realize that I'm going to have to talk to Beatty and she's going to know that I talked to you. I mean, I think I can smooth it over, but it's still probably going to get rough between you and her at work." Gail thought about it for a minute and then said "Honestly, I think she is going to be quite relieved that I told you, so she can have this terrible burden taken off of her shoulders."

"Gail, if she is uncooperative to you, do you think you might be able to get your hands on that letter long enough for me to take a look and let the lab boys take a shot at it?"

"No Thomas, that's the first time that I saw the letter and for all I know, she has it under lock and key somewhere away from the office. Here is her name and number and what floor she is on."

"Ok, I'll see what I can do about this particular situation and see if I can't come up with something that helps solve the problem." Thomas said with an air of confidence. "Now do you need a ride home?"

Thomas realized that this was finally a new lead and an angle that he never saw coming. He questioned himself as to whether he might have overlooked anything else. Although he had kept his wits about him when he talked to Gail, he wondered if there was anything else he might have asked her, that might have helped. Note to self he thought—*next time don't drink so damn much!*

He decided that he would go and visit Beatty Morgenstern on Monday and try to convince her that she share that letter with the Department and anything else that she might know. But first he wanted to make a note to update a list of possible suspects that he had created during the investigation.

Chapter 10
The Suspects

TaskForce HQ

First thing in the morning, Thomas took out that sheet of paper and jotted down additional information:

Persons of Interest in the MURDER AT TRANSIT case

BEATTY MORGENSTERN
-VP of the Developed Technologies Dept (DT)
Description: 45 year old woman, short with dark wavy hair
Work location: Transit/Waterfront
Status: Married/2 kids

WINSTON ALLCUS
-Current Employee/ Electrical Improvement Dept (EI)
Description: 53 year old man, medium build with brn hair
Work location: Transit/Waterfront
Status: Single

CARLOS ALLCUS
-Current Employee/ Material Consumption Dept (MC)
Description: 68? year old man, slight build with white hair
Work location: Transit/Waterfront
Status: Single

JIMMY 'the Shakes' WILSON
-Current Employee/light duty/ Signs&Signals Dept (SS)
Description: 52 year old man, lge build with balding head
black hair/beard
Work location: Transit/Waterfront
Status: Married/4 kids

JAMES ARRONDI
-Former Employee, Developed Technologies Dept (DT)
Description: 58 year old man, med build/dirty brn long hair
Former Work location: Transit/Waterfront
Status: Married/3 kids

MAX DORMAN
-Vendor/Consultant-various, including Transit
Description: 42 year old man, med build/short brn hair
Work location: Various
Status: Divorced/no kids

GAIL DIAZ
-Current Employee /Developed Technologies Dept (DT)
Description: 44 year old, med build/dirty blond short hair
Work location: Transit/Waterfront
Status: Unmarried

PAUL & CHARLES DORKIN
-Vendors/Consultants
Description: 62 and 63 year old men, med build/grey hair
Work location: Various
Status: both Married

LOU LONG
-Former Employee Signs&Slogans Dept (S&S)
Description: 65 year old man, lge build/dyed blk hair
Former Transit/Waterfront
Status: Married 2 or 3 kids?

SCANNER SIMMONS — DECEASED!
RON RIMSUM — DECEASED
3 JOHN DOE'S — DECEASED

Thomas thinks to himself ... Just a reminder, I've got to go and pay a visit to that fellow Long ... Lou Long. If what these guys said was true, he has enough of a grudge to want revenge, but this layoff/firing thing really had nothing to do with him, as far as I know. And besides he might just be a *total loon by now ...!*

—I've also got to do a follow-up with these guys, James Arrondi, The Dorkins and Max Dorman.

Transit

Thomas arrived at the office of Mrs. Morgenstern unannounced. As Gail led him into the room, she tried to speak to Beatty quietly.

"I thought it best ..." she started to say.

Beatty said "I understand Gail, you can leave us now and shut the door please. I recognize you, Thomas Banner."

"Hello Beatty, I'm investigating the case of The Lone Rider and I understand that you have some information that might shed a little light on the case. May I see the letter?"

"I'm sure you can understand that I no longer keep it here for fear that it might fall into the wrong hands. I'm so afraid you see."

Beatty wanted to be given some assurances that she and her family would be protected, as best as possible.

"Since, I know the content of the letter, do you have any ideas as to who might have sent it to you? I want you to be as honest as you can be with me. From what Gail has told me, I think you realize that your situation at work, is of no concern to me at this time. We just need your assistance, to help in solving this case."

"I appreciate your discretion in this matter and I will tell you all that I know and who I believe is the suspect." she said after regaining her composure.

"I'm pretty sure that it's Matt Dorland!"

"*Wait a minute*, I know that name, he was the fellow that briefed us that first day when we went to Transit headquarters. What does he have to do with any of this?" Thomas has been thrown for a loop with this revelation.

"When I first came into Transit, I came in with Matt Dorland, who I trusted and in time, when my marriage was in trouble, I turned to him—in confidence. We became lovers, but it was a short-lived thing and rumors flew around here. We were very careful and business like, and still stories circulated. Even if we were never lovers at all, the stories would have occurred because people here like to have drama at the office.

Somehow, my career flourished and I quickly rose up the company ladder. Unfortunately, Dorland's career seemed to suffer because of the rumors or at least that's how he felt. What was once a friendship, started to turn into a real competitive thing and then it started to get really ugly between us. Well, of course, I still cared for him and it really upset me to see what had happened to us."

She then took a really deep breath and said "One day years later, I met with him after work to see if we could mend our relationship and then one drink lead to another, and another. The next thing you know, we would up back in bed. That's when the next morning, he hit me up with a request to do him a huge favor, that would put everything right with him and his advancement in the company."

He said that he was in trouble, because of a gambling debt and that he had made contact with a group of people, who wanted to land a big fat contract with Transit. "All he needed" he said, "was that when it came time for some companies to put in a price for providing major hardware and software, that his people had to WIN regardless of the price they put in. Could I just once, help see to it that the bidding procedure was circumvented, by making sure only this one selected company would win. Because they were unique in terms of offering a practical solution, it could be justified!"

She continued. "I didn't know what to say. I was shocked, I was angry and *I was in love.* I was asked to go against all my principals and I eventually faltered. He made such wonderful arguments that it really didn't matter who won and that this was a reputable company, so there was nothing to worry about! (And, that he was sure that this happened all the time, at Transit.)

Well sure enough, a few months later when things started to go wrong and I kept getting asked to '*look the other way*' more, and more. Like a snowball up the hill that starts rolling down, the problems just got deeper and deeper and the solutions to the money thing started to really get out-of-hand.

Oh, and what about Matt? Well, he had a way of involving others in management, until he was so powerful that he ... wangled his way into a position of power, as the Vice Director. He was *strong* and most of those around him were *weak*. He was ruthless and he came up with all these ways to hide the money being spent and I became his unwitting accomplice. He had plans to become the next Head of Transit, but they were thwarted by those members who had their own agenda. 'Politics' always wins in cases like that.

I should mention that once he got that title, he distanced himself from me, sent me into Siberia, so to speak." she said as if wounded and hurt deeply.

"But it doesn't make sense. Why would a guy, who is after all so powerful, want to risk everything to do this and if he goes after you, he loses the main person in this scheme?"

She stood up and walked over to Thomas and said. "Because all of this is a diversion, so that he can *murder* me and silence the one person who could ruin everything for him. ***There won't be any other murders—just me!*** And *remember*, he does have quite an ego so, he also did this to see if anyone might discover the money cover-ups. he's checking to see if there's anything—he missed."

"Listen Beatty, why would he warn you? By sending you that letter, he has given you a heads-up, so why would he do that?" Beatty turned to him and said "He's just testing my loyalty and love for him. He's pretty confident that I had the inner-strength to be able to take all this pressure and not crack, not tell anyone, but I couldn't do it. Nobody could do that—*except Matt!*"

"And, what makes me so sure that he's the guilty one. Well, he was a very jealous guy and when we were in bed, he always used to ask me ... was he the only one? I always replied that he was ...

"THE LONE RIDER!"

"OK Beatty, I've taken everything you said and considered it and I'm not going to make any judgements now, but I will go see Dorland. I'd like to talk to him when he's away from headquarters. Is there anywhere, that I might be able to have a word with him, possibly alone?"

"Yes, Thomas ... on Friday night at around 10 P.M. he will be at his apartment uptown."

"How do you know this?"

"Because ... I will be there with him ... you see, I am STILL in love with him."

"Is there any other way, things might not go well there and you could be in danger Beatty!"

"No ... you see .... I want to be there to try to keep things calm between you two—and protect him from doing anything *stupid*."

"Alright, Friday night it is then." She quickly writes down the address and gives it to him.

"Good day Beatty."

Once outside the office as he is walking to the elevator, Gail runs up to him and asks how it went. "Is Beatty going to be alright and does she need to be concerned for her safety as well."

Thomas says "I don't think you have anything to worry about, but once I tell my boss about the situation, I'll have whoever is posted here, keep an eye out for you, too."

"Thank you Thomas and good luck with the investigation." She returns to her desk, where she is paged to go into Beatty's office.

Thomas leaves and gets back into his car and heads back toward his office.

Matt Dorland? Matt Dorland? I mean he's a pretty sharp guy as I recall, one of those guys who looks like he was born in a suit. He's the mastermind of this whole big mess, plus he's THE LONE RIDER?

Thomas can't help, but think back to that day at Transit ExecutiveCentr. "Now that I really think about it, man were we handed such a *ton of crap* from him. I just thought he was protecting his territory, nothing more." Thomas says out loud as if he were back talking to Joseph. If Joseph were here he would have been the one to sent to interview Dorland.

Just then, a call comes over his car radio.
"THOMAS PROCEED TO MILT'S BAR & GRILL"

"Joseph was there recently, listening to that old man telling him that he was positive, that his brother was THE LONE RIDER." Again, Thomas talks out loud. Then, he thinks to himself, if I keep talking to myself like this, they're going to put me away soon ...

Milt's

Thomas has reached Milt's and proceeds to pull into the parking lot, where he is greeted by his boss Paul Peters. "Thomas, I'm glad you're here. I have someone I want you to meet."

Thomas walks in and says hello to the bartender and to one of the waitresses he knows and then they proceed into the back room. The door is opened and all of a sudden there is very loud shout

" S U R P R I S E ! "

Inside the room, are a number of friends and family, there to greet him. Cameras are flashing and people are screaming and carrying on. Thomas was so busy at these last few months that he had forgotten that today, was his twentieth year with the Agency.

His wife Christine ran over to greet him and whispered in his ear "You do remember what you promised me Thomas, that you would put in your papers and retire darling."

It seemed that this night would last forever to him. The speeches, stories, accolades and presentations were unbelieveable. They had really pulled out all of the stops, on this one. Peters, after his speech had handed Thomas a large envelope, that contained the papers he would need to fill out to RETIRE. God, he *hated that word!* It was like you were being put out to pasture and you had no say in the matter. And what about his kids, who was going to pay for the rest of their education, if he retired? Still he had a great night.

As the evening was coming to a close, it was Thomas' turn to speak.

*"Friends and family and those of you I have worked with ... I would just like at this time, to pay my respects to those I have worked with and have fallen, I especially would like to single out my last partner **Joseph Sorelo**, he will never be forgotten. (the crowd is on their feet clapping wildly). I can only say that I tried to do my job in the best way that I know how and if that happened to included a few banged-up cars, some property damage, and a number of broken bones on the bad guys-so be it!, Sorry Peters."*

Thomas continued "One last thing, to my Christine and our kids Gary and Rick, who have put up with more than most have, I send out all of my love and gratitude. So, thank you and get home safe."

Just as Thomas was about to leave, Kimberly came over to him and handed him an envelope, she said "This came for you earlier, but I didn't want to give it to you until now, in case it was job related, Good night Thomas, what a great night it was for you and your family.

Thomas told his wife and family to head to the car and he went back inside and proceeded to open the letter. As he was opening it, he couldn't help, but reflect on what a great night it was. And to think, it was for HIS benefit. Wow! Twenty years *already!*

He opened the letter. The letter said:
"I MAY HAVE TO CONSIDER TAKING MORE THAN ONE PERSON OUT OF SERVICE ... YOU!" ... THE LONE RIDER

Thomas carefully put the letter back in its envelope. Thomas was visibly shaken. How could anyone, other than those he trusted, know that he would be here tonight? And, why would he now be threatened, unless he was being followed and he/she knew that he had been to see Beatty earlier today.

Thomas was unusually quiet on the short ride back home. He attributed it to his having had a really long day and a couple of drinks in him. Luckily, Christine was driving. He was asleep on the way home, when all of a sudden a car heading in the opposite lane—*seemed to head directly towards their car.*

She swerved just in time to miss hitting that car, but their car was side-swiped and she headed into a ditch and hit a tree. Everybody was alright and luckily, she had managed to slow down enough, so that she only slightly damaged the car. In the instant before the accident, Thomas had awaken and managed to notice that the last numbers of the license plate were 7-4-2-5 as the car passed by.

Christine said to Thomas "It was really odd, it felt like that car *deliberately* headed towards us. Why would anyone do such a thing? Probably just some idiot, talking on their cell-phone or something."

Thomas on the other hand, had quite different thoughts. I'm sure that was no *accident* he thought to himself. That probably was the same guy who sent the letter. If he/she's been watching me, that makes a lot of sense. Well, in the morning, I'll have that plate run and see if anything turns up.

TaskForce HQ

The next day at work, Thomas went into the office and had the plate checked. Kimberly stopped by as soon as she got into work and asked about the letter. Thomas looked up at her and said "It was nothing really, just an informant with a piece of news about another case. But thanks for remembering to give it to me. By the way I hope you had a great time last night. Luckily, the party broke-up pretty early, because everyone had work the next day."

"I had such a nice time. You have such a really nice family and Christine is just amazing. You truly are indeed a very lucky man Thomas."

It was then that Thomas noticed a large envelope on his desk. He knew it was another copy of his **Retirement papers**, left there no doubt by his boss. He knew his boss really didn't want him to go, but since he was a diehard by-the-book kind of guy, this was not unexpected.

About an hour later, Kimberly walks in with a report on that plate that he requested info on. Turns out it came from a late model red Cruiser that belonged to, of all people, CARLOS ALLCUS!

[He knew the car was red, because he had red paint on the side of his car, where it scrapped his.]

I think I'm going to have to pay Carlos a visit ...

"Excuse me Thomas, it's Kimberly again. There's a call for you on line 2"

"Hello, Special Agent Thomas Banner. How can I help you?"

"You can help yourself, by staying totally out of my business. I know you have a wife and two children that you love. You wouldn't want anything to happen to them, like what almost happened to them last night ... CLICK!"

Thomas didn't recognize the voice, it was very muffled, but it wasn't Carlos Allcus, that I'm sure of. This one spoke too quickly!

Again he was stumped. Were there two people following me? Were they working together? How many more twists and turns were going to happen with this case? So many questions Thomas thought ...

Just then Kimberly walked in. "Thomas there's been an update on one of the people that you guys interviewed. Seems you need to go down to the morgue. It appears that Carlos Allcus is dead, and it appears to be a suicide!"

The old man a suicide-NO WAY!

The old man a suicide-NO WAY!

The old man a suicide-NO WAY!

It just continued to echo in his brain ...

Chapter 11
The Stiff

Morgue

Thomas arrived at the morgue later that day and saw the remains of Mr. Allcus.

The coroner said "It appears that this 73 year old white male apparently hung himself with his own necktie, when he leapt over a bannister. Though he weighed a mere 105 pounds, his weight and the force of the fall, was enough to snap his neck. We are going to do an autopsy, because, it also appears that he put up quite a struggle, as he has bruises on his body, two of his fingers were broken on his right hand and there is blood and fibers underneath his fingernails. He also has a contusion on the back of his head, but that probably was the result of his head hitting the staircase, after he jumped or was pushed."

"How long do you think he's been dead?" Thomas asked knowing full well that after all this time, he had a pretty good idea.

"I can't say for sure until the lab results come back, but I'd say he's been dead over 48 hours or more."

Thomas thought to himself, then who the heck was driving the car, that almost killed my family and myself? It certainly wasn't him. So, it seems more than likely it was ... THE LONE RIDER or an accomplice ...

Just then a Detective entered the room. "I'm Detective Kip Slinger and you are ..."

"I'm Special Agent Thomas Banner, I'm working on The Lone Rider case and this was one of the people that I've interviewed."

"Well Banner, it might interest you to know that whoever did this to him, gave his place a through going over. What's even more interesting is that the IDENTICAL apartment *next door* to his place, was tossed too. Seems like someone put a lot of effort into doing all that."

"What do you mean 'identical'."

"I mean identical like everything in the apartment was an *exact duplicate*, right down to the silverware. Seems there was an adjoining door that led from one apartment to the other. It was located inside the master closet in both apartments."

"Slinger, you mind if I take a look around those apartments for myself?"

"Be my guest Banner, but you won't find anything. The place was searched upside down by the uniform guys, our guys, and the murderer. Anyhow, here's the address.

"So, you don't think it was a suicide *either*?"

"I think we'll wait for the autopsy report before we make it official, but I've been doing this long enough to..."

"Thanks Detective, I'll be in touch, if you find out anything else, here's my card."

Allcus apartments

Thomas heads on over to the apartment and shows his ID and is allowed into the Apartment on the left side. He looks around, very carefully, as not to disturb the crime scene. Since the police photographer has already been here and the place has been dusted for prints, he walks around the apartment trying to notice and take in as much detail as possible. He always prided himself on his *powers of observation*. Next, he enters the other apartment through the door in the master closet.

Again, he walks around the apartment, looking for anything that might be slightly out of place. It *appears* that everything is exactly the same. Of course, everything has been thrown around, still everything is identi ...

"Wait a minute what's this!?" he says out loud. Thomas could not help but notice, that hanging on each living room wall above the couch, was a rather large painting of late 18th century interior work/study room. The painting was done in a super-realistic manner. The pictures appear to be identical works, by the same artist! It's uncanny how the two pictures can look so exact ...

HOWEVER ... on the desk in each painting, are a number of letters, addressed to various people—except that one letter on the corner of the desk is addressed to *Matt Dorland!* And, on the other painting, the letter on the corner is addressed to:

THE ANVIL 2 CONCRETE COMPANY
—and the stamps on these letters appear to be a modern ones. These paintings are AMAZING and so realistic ....

The other thing that seemed out of place was on the bookshelf, which seemed to contain rather normal fare. Biographies, Stamps and Mystery books etc., there was one on RARE ELEMENTS. He walked over and picked up that book and leafed through it and what do you know, a section in the book had been highlighted. Thomas carefully read those paragraphs that were highlighted. One section in particular caught his eye. That section was entitled:

ZINIUM: *The section highlight included where it could be found. Also a comparison chart of its value and usefulness, then and now.*

An additional paragraph or two mentioned how rare it now was compared to other elements. Turns out that there were two Rare Element books that were highlighted, *one in each apartment.*

And, wasn't that the stuff that they used for that special collectible ClickCard? Thomas realized that his work at these apartments was done.

On the drive back to the office, Thomas is thinking about why those paintings at the Allcus apartments were different. Perhaps this was his way of protecting himself should anything go wrong. Maybe, I'll take a ride over to see Winston Allcus and see if I can get any information from him, regarding the death of his brother. Then, Thomas remembers that he needed to kill some time, before he goes to Dorland's. He needs to get Uptown by around 10 P.M.

Dorland's apartment

Thomas arrives 10 minutes after 10 P.M. Friday night. He goes inside. He hears some arguing inside the apartment. It's about 10:15 when he rings the doorbell and is let in by Beatty.

[*This apartment duplex on the Upper West Side is extremely opulent—Apparently, he must come from money or his money must come from other sources.*]

"This is rather unusual Banner. Do you make it a habit of working such late hours?" Dorland said and then he gave Thomas a look of disapproval.

"I'm just trying to do my job." Thomas walks over to the fireplace and picks up a very ornate vase.

"Careful Banner, that vase is worth *considerably more* than you make in a year." Still holding on to the vase, Thomas asks Dorland a question. He is paying close attention to how Dorland reacts ...

"So where were you around 10 P.M. on Wednesday evening? You wouldn't happen to have be out for a drive, were you?"

"So, would you like a drink Banner? Beatty please pour me a double Scotch and Soda. Thank you!" He then takes a sip of his drink and walks over to the fireplace where Banner is standing.

"I was here with Beatty that night and I never left her for a moment. Isn't that true Beatty? And please put down that vase Banner." Thomas complies with the request. He has a hunch that Beatty was put up to say that he was with her, but she doesn't want to say that now.

"You didn't come all the way over here to ask what I was doing the other night. What's really on your mind. Oh! And I know you and Beatty had a conversation about me and Transit business. She has told me ALL about it. Keep in mind that we have been investigated, a number of times. And we're all still here!"

"Well truth be told, from what she's told me, there's a lot of stuff that has been going on and it appears to be emanating from you. So the question I have to ask you is..."

"Are you THE LONE RIDER?"

"NO! I certainly am not!" Dorland said unequivocally.

"And I resent you asking me that question. A man in my position has to make tough decisions everyday, on a wide variety of matters. I have been given this huge responsibility of trying to turn this organization in a new direction.

I'm a critical part of policy decisions, product enhancements and a million other things. What makes you think a man in my position, no matter how *compromised*—would resort to murder, when I have the power to affect lives in so many other ways." He finishes the rest of his drink in one swallow.

"No matter what Beatty may have told you, her virtues were compromised, long before she came to Transit. Do you know how I first came to meet Beatty? Tell him Beatty dear."

"No, No I can't ... I won't—don't make me Matt. Please don't tell him."

"Well Banner, I *will* tell you. I had just gotten out of the Navy. I first met Beatty when I was twenty-three. You see there was this house around Midtown, on the West Side. You know the kind of house that a sailor or multiple numbers of sailors, might want to go to." He walks up really close to Thomas now.

"Well, I'm ushered upstairs to a beautiful room, where Beatty is entertaining the troops, she had taken on a number of fellas at once!" Beatty starts to sob uncontrollably.

"THAT'S ENOUGH DORLAND!"

"So you see Banner, if I wanted to ruin her life, there are certain facts that I could make well known to Transit, to the Public and especially to her *husband*. I really don't need to murder her or anyone, now do I?" Dorland looked over at Beatty who was still sobbing.

"Beatty and I have no secrets because what she knows about me and what I know about her *kind of cancel each other out*. Anyhow the hour is getting late so, unless you have any other questions Banner, I think Beatty and I will go back to bed."

"I do have one more question for now. What's it like to come across someone who's not afraid of you?" Thomas walked to the door and then turned around and said.

"If I find anything that suggests that you are looking to do me or my family harm *I will find you* and I will take you down ... —Goodnight, Beatty."

"Banner, I lied to you!" Dorland says to him as he continues to stroke Beatty's hair. Thomas turns back in his direction to listen.

"That vase was worth considerably more than you'll ever make in your lifetime."

Banner slams the door on the way out, then opens it again.

"I will be stopping in to see you again at your job or here and I will expect your full cooperation." Banner slams the door again. Dorland thinks to himself that his neighbors, are just going to love him ... He turns to Beatty and says "THANK GOD he didn't drop that vase."

All the way on the ride home, he can't figure out why Beatty has such loyalty to such a creep as Dorland. All the while she's leading two separate lives.

One with her husband and family and one with HIM!

Chapter 12
The Heist

TaskForce HQ

Thomas is back at his desk, after what seemed like a really long weekend with his family. For once he was able to relax and unwind and enjoy, without spending to much time thinking about the Murder at Transit case. As he settles back in his desk, he goes over the number of murders that have occurred that are or might be linked to this case already. He makes a list:

Deceased

Joseph Sorelo
Scanner Simmons
Ronald Rimsum
(& 2 men and a woman)
Carlos Allcus

Thomas starts to get back into his investigation. This Carlos thing doesn't sit well with him at all. According to the notes I found in Joseph's car, after he was murdered, he said that Scanner had found tens of thousands of dollars and some report about substandard concrete. I'm thinking that the ANVIL2 CONCRETE COMPANY is somehow involved in this and may provide another lead.

Just then, Senior Agent Paul Peters walks in and says to him,
"I left an envelope on your desk a couple of weeks ago and I still haven't seen those papers come across my desk Banner. When are you going to...?"
"Look Peters, you know I want to see the Murder at Transit case through to the end. So, I'll make a deal with you. Let me finish out that investigation and take me off the rest of my workload. If you do that, I promise to ... reti ... *leave* right after that."
Unbeknownst to Thomas Banner, that was exactly what Peters had wanted him to do.

"I'll do that on two conditions:

First:
"You put in the papers by the end of the week
—just leave the final date BLANK."

Second:
"You bring the staff up to speed on the other cases and you do what ever is necessary, turn over any leads, give a deposition, whatever it takes to finish up ...
—UNDERSTOOD."

"Paul, you know what I like about you NOW?"
"Yeah, Yeah I do. ***Everything!***"

"And you have a visitor, waiting outside your office for you, I'll send him in." Peters walks out and motions for someone to go in.
"Mr. Drake! Long time no see buddy. How is the grimy world of reporting nowadays? I mean after there was a Fifty Thousand Dollar reward, I thought for sure that someone would have turned up something, by now." Thomas says that with a really quizzical look on his face.
"Turns out that I've been doing some digging on my own and it seems like 'fifty big ones' is chicken-feed!"
"How so?" Thomas asked, in mock amazement.
"Turns out it's much more lucrative to find whoever has that Zinium collectible ClickCard. Seems no one can prove who made the threat in the Murder at Transit case, but the word on the street is that Card is worth *MILLIONS!*"

And you're going to love this ... Christopher said "Turns out that Rimsum at one point thought he knew where the card was located. That's why he had those uniforms. He broke into a Transit location he used to visit, back when he was tagging trains as a kid.
Apparently Transit hasn't worked on securing that location YET! Anyhow, he put together a crew who was planning to pull a heist over at the Anvil2 Concrete Company when his van ran into yours. So how do you like that news my friend?"

"When did you find this out and why didn't you bring this information to me sooner, Christopher?"

"You know Thom, sometimes the street takes its time before it gives up any information."

"So Christopher what do you know about the Anvil2 Company?"

"It turns out that right after they started to print some of those Collectible ClickCards, they had some financial problems.

Something to do with submitting bills to Transit and because of some serious **computer meltdown**—they were not getting paid on time ... this continued for almost as long as the Collectible program existed. Then, Transit got some new computer equipment. —*problem solved*!

"Anything else on Anvil2?"

"Thomas, the only other thing I know about them is that they were a pretty legit place, until some new silent partners took over and then things started to change."

Seems they held on to the company until that Collectible Card program finished and then they shut it down."

"Would you happen to know where that printing company was located?"

"Yeah, it was in the same building, as the Anvil2 company."

"Thanks for the info Drake and by the way, you still haven't brought any donuts? Peters keeps asking for them ...!"

"What a wiseguy. So, what have you got for me, my friend?"

"Well, I seem to have tons of information and possibly a suspect who's pretty high up in Transit management. So, do you have any background or info on a guy named Matt Dorland?"

"He's a real *slickster* from all accounts, born with a silver spoon in his mouth. His families been in the Public eye forever. The National stage is their calling. I think that his family was a little disappointed, that instead of going into Politics, he choose Public Service—and Transit at that! I hear he's a tough son-of-a bitch when he's negotiating."

"Yeah, that's just about my impression of him too."

"Well thanks again Christopher. if I turn anything else up I'll let you know."

Thomas grabs his coat and heads out the door. He figures it's about time to go visit the Anvil2 Company.

Chapter 13
The List

Anvil2 company

Thomas turns up the next morning, at the entranceway, to what appears to be a bustling company. The loading dock is active, as are the concrete mixing trucks that are preparing to deliver their contents. Thomas goes inside the open door and proceeds upstairs to an office full of people taking orders or filling them.

He approaches a door in the back and just as he's about to go in, out comes of all people, Detective Slinger!

"Small world ain't it Banner."

"I'd a thought you were following me Slinger, but you got here first, so that can't be right."

"The fellow you want to talk to is the guy in the corner by the big window. Names Jesse Knight, he's the Boss."

"Thanks Slinger, anything more on that Allcus case?"

"Just what you read in the papers, I guess. Hey Jesse, this is Special Agent Thomas Banner—wants to ask you a couple of questions ..."

"Listen Banner, as you can see I'm a very busy man. So, make it quick."

"Is there somewhere we can go an talk?" Thomas asks.

"Alright, the coffee wagon just rang the bell outside so, let's get a cup of coffee. I needed a break anyway" said Knight.

Thomas is interested in how long he's been here, what kind of clients do they serve and more importantly does he have any records on the printing company that they shut down.

"Well, we've been making *cement shoes* ... just kidding! I've owned it for twenty years and we service the construction industry. From the little guy, through to the major corporations. "Do you ever do work for State and City agencies?" Thomas wants to know.

"We don't do much of that stuff anymore, there's no money in it. Also, it takes to long to get a contract, approvals or be paid."

Thomas asks, "by any chance did you know or do business with a fellow named Carlos Allcus."

"Can't say that, that name rings a bell." Knight says.

"Apparently he was familiar enough with your company to have

81

its name and address added onto a customized painting he had hanging in his apartment. Seems a little *odd*, dont you think?"

Knight took a moment to absorb where this conversation was going ... He didn't like the direction. He cut Banner off and said "Listen if there's anything else you want to talk to me about, you're going to have to do it through my lawyer. And that's all I'm going to say for now."

"OK, we can go that route if you want, but I would advise you to stick around for awhile."

As Thomas was getting into his car, a worker with a slight accent walked up behind him and says:

"Meet me at the Eskimo diner, right down the road from Anvil2. I have something very important to talk to you about."

Eskimo diner

Thomas waited for this fellow to show. He was sure taking his time. Thomas was just about to leave, when in walks a man that looked directly at him and then all around, as if to see if anyone else he knew was there. He sat down across from Thomas and introduced himself.

"My name is Hans Questhammer. I'm a materials specialist at Anvil2 and I work for a Mr. Knight. I wanted to talk to someone about what has been going on in this company."

"Why talk to me? Why didn't you just talk to Detective Slinger? I'm sure he could help you, no matter what is troubling you."

"No, I can't. Because ... he's in on it. He's on the *take*, as a matter of fact, he roughed-up three workers and then the next thing you know—one of them completely disappears."

"Three workers are roughed-up and one disappears you say? Listen Questhammer, The truth is I'm only here to get additional information on whether a Carlos Allcus had anything to do with this company and if anyone knows about some concrete used on a job that *wasn't up to standard*. Do you know anything about any of this?"

"Yes, Yes I do. It is my job to submit samples to the companies or organizations, before we can proceed to deliver we have to pour a sample. They then run some additional tests and then the approval or denial is issued."

So, did you ever work with Carlos Allcus?"

"No, but he would show up to the office from time to time and argue with Slinger. One night I stayed really late and there was some big meeting going on in the conference room. It must have been around 10 o'clock. I was working in my office, trying to catch up on some paperwork and as I left for the evening I saw a light on in the conference room. And I heard some really loud arguing. Anyway, as I moved closer to the room and I noticed that the door was not fully closed and I saw all of them in there."

"Did you know who they were. Do you know their names?"

"I didn't then, but I do now. I wrote them down on this list for you." He hands Thomas the paper with the following names on it...

Jesse Knight
Carlos & Winston Allcus
Kip Slinger
Charlie & Paul Dorkins
Betty Morgenstern
Matt Dorland
Doc Redin

Thomas is blown away because he never expected to know most of the names on the list.

"Did you have any idea what the meeting was about? Did they talk about a particular project or job that they were working on."

"Yes, several times during the meeting they mentioned a project that had been beset by problems, from tile-work done without including the name of the place in the tiles, to a plague of leaks. Carlos said that the situation was unsafe and that *lives could be lost* eventually, if things were not corrected now! By what they said, I could only conclude that they were talking about some special project. Dorland, at one point, was defending the fact that Transit had committed to having a press conference tour, way before the final construction on the place, was actually finished.

When it looked like they were going to leave the meeting, I scrambled to get out, without anyone seeing me."

"Do you know who Doc Redin is or what company he works for? Or if he's a real doctor?"

"I got that list from Knights receptionist Rosemarie, she and I have been dating for awhile. After I described those in attendance, she was able to give me that list. Doc Redin? I don't know who he is or what he was doing there? I do know that he didn't say very much throughout the meeting."

"There are some more things I'd like to ask you, but I have to get back. Here's my card, call me in a few days to meet with me again. Thanks again, Hans" Thomas now feels he has a terrific lead with this new information. His confidence is building back slowly.

Chapter 14
The Truth?

Butley's

Thomas heads over to Butley's and sits down at the booth and has a beer. He needs to make sense of what he has recently learned. And he has questions, lots of questions. Who is Doc Redin? What could all of those characters on that list be involved in? What is really going on with Morgenstern and Dorland?

It turns out that Beatty seems to be inconsistent with the story she been putting forth:

Originally, she tells Diaz that she is afraid that Dorland is the main suspect and she's in fear of her life because of him.

On the other hand ...

She tells me to meet her at *his* apartment and the next thing I find out is that she's attending a meeting late at night with him. If she's so afraid of him, why would she spend so much time with him and also say that he is THE LONE RIDER?

then again ...

She told Diaz that the order to buy that computer equipment, it must have come from upstairs at Transit yet, she told me that he asked her to do it.

I think she's covering up something else!

And then there's the part of her being a hooker in her younger days, doesn't surprise me. But that they've know each other for over twenty years—I guess that does buy you a lot of loyalty.

Thomas thinks to himself, I know that Dorland's up to his neck in dirty deeds, but by protecting his position with intimidation, he's opened himself up to someone spilling there guts about him. Still could he really be the one?

Another thing that troubles him about this investigation is the fact that Winston Allcus would be at that meeting. He didn't strike me as someone that would be involved in any of this.

Still this investigation has taken more twists and turns than I ever could have imagined and I'm still no closer to the answer, than when I started this case. And I'm running out of time. I still have a few more leads to track down. And I still have to find out who was driving Carlos Allcus' car when my family and I were almost all killed?

Thomas thinks to himself, ever since I thought someone might be following me, I've kept an eye out for anything suspicious. I still haven't noticed anyone following me, but I'm still going to keep my guard up,

[*Thomas is unaware that someone has put a tracking device in the official car that he's been driving and his family car.*]

Thomas orders another beer and figures that he will leave when that one is finished. A few minutes later who should walk into the bar and sit down across from him at his booth, but Kip Slinger.

"Agent Banner just thought we might have a drink together."

"I already have a beer." Thomas says

"Well then I'll have a drink. Waiter, bring me a beer."

"So what's on your mind. I'm sure you didn't stop in here just to make a social call. And how did you know where to find me?"

"I am a Detective remember. Finding out about stuff is my business. Finding out about people is also my business. Now as it turns out you and I have a mutual acquaintance, we might want to talk about."

"And just who might that be?"

" Mr. Matt Dorland."

"Don't know that there's anything about him that I might want to talk to you about Slinger." Thomas looks at him as if to say —don't go there.

"Listen Banner, don't give me any of your attitude! I'm just here to give you a little helpful advice..." Both men are now standing beside the booth. Each man is sizing the other up and the situation is getting more tense by the moment ...

"And what might that advice be Slinger?"

"During your investigation you might want to consider that your checking out some of the wrong people and one of them is Matt Dorland ... SO BACK OFF!"

"Oh! So that's who's calling your tune now."
"What do you mean by that remark?"
"You KNOW what I meant."
"Well I don't like your attitude..."

Boom!

Slinger swings towards Banner and hits him on the jaw which knocks him down. He gets up and tackles Slinger and they spin around and over to the bar, knocking over glasses and barstools.

More punches are exchanged before the bouncer separates the two of them. "If you want to fight, take it outside!"

Both men dust themselves off and Slinger says "That's enough for now, but heed my warning—BACK THE FUCK OFF!"
Banner looks at him. shakes his head back and forth and says "Do you really think that what you say is going to prevent me from doing my job?"
"Just remember this isn't finished Banner." he then turns and walks away. Thomas says "This is just getting STARTED!"
He then sits back down and orders another beer. And he says to himself "Man, that Detectives got some right cross ..."

Now, Dorland must be getting a little worried, if he has to send a goon like that to come and harass me. So it appears to me that there's really no other reason for Dorland to have done this unless he is or has something to do with the *Murder at Transit* case.

Chapter 15
The Max

TaskForce HQ

"Gee, every time I think that time is standing still, it just whizzes by me—fast as blazes." Thomas says to himself in a soft whisper.

Thomas eventually receives a short call from his new buddy Hans Questhammer, who says he's gotten more information.

Eskimo diner

Thomas sits waiting for Hans to come in. As usual he is running late. Finally he walks in, looks around and then sits down again in a booth with Thomas. He has a large folder with him.

"Agent Banner I just found out that it looks like those people on the list are going to have another meeting ... I think you should be there too. And I think I've found a way to listen in, without being discovered."

"When is the next meeting Hans?

"Tomorrow night."

"That's just great." Thomas says "I also managed to do some research into who this Doc Redin fellow is. Apparently, he's the fellow who owned the printing company that Anvil bought, the one that used the Zinium material in the Collectible ClickCard."

"You're right, I discovered that information also, when I went and snuck into the closed-off part of the building where they printed. There was a door that just needed a little persuasion to open, and I was able to look at a number of records and such.

I wanted to give you this folder and see if it helps you any way with your investigation. I did notice that a number of files seemed to be missing, like someone had broken into these files before I had a chance to." As for the computer equipment they had, the stuff was so old, I didn't know how to access it."

"Well let me just take a little peak into what's here in this folder. That's funny, it does looks like somebody switched some stuff around. I'll check into it in detail later, but this is great stuff Hans."

"In case I didn't make this quite clear, I just don't want my name associated with anything that is going to hurt anyone. I'm pretty sure that someone forged my signature on documents that OK'ed the concrete that was not up to standard. I don't want to be held responsible for the deaths of anyone on my conscience."

"What do you mean deaths?"

"Thomas sir, if a structure is built with weak material—it's just a matter of time before it *crumbles* ...

"I still have to check on what projects that involves, as you said there were several you were working on, at the time. I will notify the proper authorities. after I get some more information. I am going to leave now, but you say I should meet you near the West corner of the building tomorrow night at around 9:30 P.M. ..."

TaskForce HQ

Thomas sat at his desk looking at the calendar knowing that he only has two months left on that September 17, 2011 deadline. He has gone over the case a million times in his head. There's something there that's obvious, that he's missed.

In the course of the investigation there are some people who he has never called in for an interview:

Max Dorman
[*He was previously investigated as a possible suspect in the death of Scanner Simmons and Agent Joseph Sorelo (he had an ironclad alibi for the evening of the shooting.) Banner had been given a transcript of the interview conducted and he had read it.*]
Lou Long
[*He had been investigated by Transit security soon after the threat had surfaced. He was considered too unstable at the time to have been a credible suspect. He has been in and out of medical facilities since then. He is considered dangerous to himself and others.*]
James Arrondi
[*He along with two other partners have formed a company to start printing books including ones about Transit. He has stated for the record that he expects to be sued because of them, He is still very paranoid when it comes to the organization.*]

After, Thomas makes a call to a Mr. Dorman, he arrives at the office about an hour later. He explains to Thomas that "He will be out of town for the next couple of days."

"Thank you for coming in Mr. Dorman. I just wanted to take this opportunity to ask you about your relationship with Scanner Simmons and the nature of your business with Winston Allcus?"

"You should get in touch with Detective Slinger, I've already answered those questions Banner.

Listen Dorman, you can make that flight like you want or you can wind-up staying here and missing it. The choice is yours. I just want to hear your version of it from you and not from some report."

"Alright! What do you need to know."

"How did you meet Ms. Simmons? How long did you have a relationship for? And, who in your option do you think killed her and my partner—if it wasn't you?

"First off, *I didn't kill them*." He paced back and forth as he spoke. "I meet her in the neighborhood, we went out from time to time, had a couple of laughs. Yeah, she was a girl you could really have a fun time with. Eventually, we broke up when I was transferred to another state for a while. I know she did take up with an associate of mine named Mr. Allcus. That's about it."

"And, you had no dealings with her after that?"

"No, the next thing I know is that she was murdered and her picture was in all the papers. What a shame, poor kid."

"So, your telling me that she takes up with Allcus and you weren't the least bit *upset* about that? Is that what you expect me to believe? Come on, you spent time with her, had relations with her and you're telling me you just didn't give a crap? You can do better than that Max."

"Look the Scanner I knew, knew what she was doing, she could hold her own with any man. If she saw a better opportunity she jumped at it and who could blame her. Still, three in the chest, is *a pretty hard way to go ....!*"

"Ok, Fine. What was your business with Allcus?"

"We had an interest in Transit collectibles and went on several trips looking for things to add to our collections. Sometimes we sold things that we had acquired earlier or traded-up for something that was desirable.

"So what company did you work for? I understand that you consulted on occasion for Transit. Is that true?"

"I was in business for myself under the company name of Max/Solutions. I consulted with a zillion different companies that need specialty components, printing substrates, new and unique materials, and sourcing resources."

"Did you ever hear of something called Zinium?"

90

Chapter 16
The Meeting

TaskForce HQ

Dorman keep looking at his watch. he knows that he only has a few minutes left before he needs to leave to catch his flight.

"Look Banner, I need to get out of here, so I'm going to give it to you straight. Zinium, I'm the guy that imported the stuff from overseas. They discovered this stuff and couldn't find a use for it. It cost a small fortune to get it into a form that could be extracted and then implanted in a substrate. I'm the one that talked Transit into using it, to make their collectible one-off ClickCard. You know the card that 'CLICKs' when you go through a turnstile. I lost a ton of money on that job. So many carrying charges and the like. Still it helped put my company on the map, so to speak." He looked at his watch again.

"Look Banner, I've got to get out of here like now!"
"Alright Dorman for now, just one more question. Do you have any idea who might have that Card in their possession?"

"What do you think I've been doing for the last couple of years. I've been looking to find that Card. Matt Dorland or others seem to have thwarted me at every turn. But it's still not over and I still have a chance at it.

"Alright Dorman, go on, get out of here and keep me posted if you find it."

Later that evening Banner prepares to head over and meet with Hans Questhammer. He hopes that this meeting will clarify a few questions that are still on his mind.

Will one of the people in that room be THE LONE RIDER?

He begins to wonder that maybe they are all involved in chasing that Collectible Card? Or, Maybe they are trying to devise a way of absolving themselves of blame because of the use of substandard concrete?

Or, is this just another one of those wild goose chases that he's gone on, because of this Murder at Transit case?

Anvil

Thomas appears right on time and meets Hans. They go around the back and go up two flights of stairs and enter a large storage room. Hans quietly moves through the room with his flashlight, with Banner right behind him. He gently moves aside a couple of lightweight cartons and on the floor is a one foot by one foot grill near one corner of the room. He motions to Thomas to get on the floor and listen through the grating.

He explains to Thomas "They should arrive shortly, just make sure you are absolutely quiet ...

If they should discover that we are here, our only way out is by going down past them. If we go up, our only choice is to jump in the river or we will be trapped on the roof ... OK, here they come —*be very quiet!*"

[*One by one they arrive, no more then five minutes late for any of them. There are only two problems with this situation, Thomas thinks to himself. First, the floors have such high ceilings in such an old building that it's very difficult to hear anyone, unless they speak in a much louder voice then they are now. The other problem is that there are three other people in this meeting that he's not sure he knows about. And, one of them is a woman ...*

One thing is for sure is that Dorland is in charge of the meeting and Slinger is his enforcer.]

Thomas hears some of what Dorland is saying:

"You understand that because of_____developments,____
we know___ no choice, but to _____ _____ ____ and take matters into ___own hands. I've instructed Slinger to_____ by the Waterfront and finally do what is requir....

"Wait just a min_te Matt, I've done more than my fair share. If I have to do more than it____gonna cost_____."

"There's no need to shout Slinger. I think we _____should ____these new members to our Ring ... On my right____
is____ Mrs. Askins and to her right is J___ Ford and across from them is Ravi Singh. each____ and Mrs. Askins ____a unique piece ____the puzzle ... With any lu___we _____able to find out ____because it will allow_____to complete____the _____task soon! We need_____to_____do_____sometime.

AHHH CHEW!!!
At that very moment, the dusty room has caused Thomas to sneeze loud enough for those in the conference room below to hear!

Boom! Boom! ALL OF A SUDDEN SHOTS RING OUT!

Slinger has fired up at the ceiling, as all hell brakes loose. Some of those inside have run to the door to confront whomever is upstairs, with Slinger in the lead. Others have taken off to escape and are running out of the building.

In the meantime, Thomas and Hans run towards the exit and make a split-second decision to run *upstairs* towards the roof. Slinger gets to the stairs first and fires off some shots that just miss the two of them. Just as he is about to pursue them up the stairs, Dorland yells up to him to ...

"STOP!"

"THERE ARE TWO OF THEM AND I CAN GET THEM —THEY HAVE NOWHERE ELSE TO GO...!" Slinger pleads.

"No, I need your help now, Beatty has fallen and hurt herself. It doesn't matter about them, they really didn't overhear anything. Relax, we have nothing to fear from them.

Whoever they are, they're not important now. Come on Slinger we need to get away from here, before anyone they might have summoned, shows up. Oh! and Slinger, by the way, apparently you roughed up the wrong three employees!"

Thomas and Hans sit on the roof for a while and think how lucky they were to have gotten out of that jam. At least Hans can go back to work tomorrow, as if nothing has happened. Thomas now knows that there are three others involved in this ring including, possibly the widow of Arthur Askins, the man run over by that fast moving train ...

"Well I guess they won't be meeting here anymore Hans."

"I'm not sure I heard the names right. I think he said Something Ford and Singh." Hans still had a puzzled look on his face when he said, "Yes, I think that's right. Isn't it Thomas."

"Yes a Ravi Singh and a J. Ford." Tomorrow when I get back to the office I will check my sources and see if I can come up with anything on those two.

TaskForce HQ

Thomas checked his files on his visits to Transit and then on the Askins case, and it did mention in them that there were TWO Mrs. Askins. One that lived here and one in Kingston, Jamaica.

He then called Drake to see if he had heard of either of the three new members of what he is calling the 'Ring". Drake stated that

"He would put his ear to the ground and that the Ford name shouldn't be hard to find out about, but the Singh name was way to common and would take much longer."

Thomas normally would have considered contacting the head of security, like he did to have set-up interviews here, but he didn't trust the fellow. He felt that his loyalties were probably to Dorland and he didn't want to tip him off.

Thomas was just about to leave and contact someone else on his list when a call came through from Questhammer.

"Hey Hans, What's on your mind?"

"Well, I think I have some good news for you. I believe that, that fellow Singh, works for Transit! ... I remember now that he was the fellow that was one of the engineers on a different project that I worked on for Transit. He was very good at his job and very smart. The reason I didn't remember it right away, was that we played a lot of phone tag and there were also a number of Singh's that I was working with at the time. But only one was an R. Singh. I checked some paperwork and on one of the documents it was signed *Ravi Singh*."

"Hans that's great stuff, but did he work on that project with the bad concrete Huh? That would have put him a little closer to the 'fire' so to speak."

"But Thomas this fellow might have acted as an advisor on that project or maybe they needed an engineer for whatever they have planned?"

"Thomas hangs up the phone and as soon as he does, he gets a call from his friend Drake."

"Hey Thom, I hear there was a little excitement over at the Anvil company last night—shots fired etc—know anything about it?"

"Know anything about it? Yeah, I was in the thick of it. Seemed like it was just a group of friends having a party."

Drake knew that this meant that whatever had happen that Thomas was involved with, was part of his investigation. And, he would let Drake know as soon as he had something, before his publishing deadline.

Chapter 17
The Inquiry

Transit

Thomas looks up a name on the directory and as luck would have it there is only one R. Singh listed in this building. And he is on the 28th floor, rm 28 and his title says Senior Engineer,

"Excuse Mr. Singh, My name is Special Agent Banner with the TaskForce and I'm in the building just checking some leads. I was wondering if you might have a couple of minutes free to talk?"

Singh turns to the two employees he was meeting with and says "Alright we'll continue with this review after lunch. What is the nature of your inquiry and do you have any Identification, please."

Thomas complies with his request.

"The nature of my inquiry might start with how did you hurt your hand? (His hand has been tapped up) And, where were you last night, say about 10 P.M.?"

"I hurt my hand working at home and I was with my family last night, all night, but why do you ask?"

Thomas isn't sure if he's lying ...

"Nevermind, I'm interested to know what type of work you do. Do you work with testing materials? Concrete and such?"

"Yes, that's right, but how do you know that?" Singh is *amazed* that he would have any idea about what he does.

"So what major types of projects have you worked on, in say the last year or two?"

"I and my staff have worked on several major projects either under development or already completed. Did you have anything in particular in mind?"

"No Singh, nothing in particular. Let me ask you this. Do you have a preferred vendor list of those who supply concrete and other materials on those kind of jobs?

"Sure, I have some preferences as to type, quality and on-time delivery. Of course, it's not up to me. There is a whole process as far as who is selected."

"Do you ever work with a vendor know as the Anvil2 Concrete Company. And, if so, what do you think of their work?"

"Sir, yes I have worked with this vendor from time to time and vendors like Calcutta and Johnson & Dorkin. Different vendors are chosen based on price, quality, the type of job or the cubic yardage. Many, many things go into the decision. Anvil2 is no better or worse than any of the others. In these tough times, they cut corners like all the others."

"What do you mean 'cut-corners'? Singh, what are you trying to say ..."

"Sir, they all on occasion will send samples where the quality is first rate and then in trying to meet the deadline or due to a timing issue for the material, the quality from one load to the next may be suspect. You have to be on top of them all the time to ensure that the job is done safely and properly."

"So, your saying there would be no way that an entire job could consist of substandard material? And, you are further stating that as far as you know, there has been no construction job finished in the last year or two in which that type of situation could occur?"

"Again sir, what you say is true. There has been no job that I or anyone else here might have worked on, in which it would be allowed to occur. We have may policies and procedures to ensure that what we do remains as safe as humanly possible."
Singh is adamant about the answers he has given to Thomas.

"Once again sir. Am I under suspicion for a crime? Are you accusing me of anything criminal?"

"Not at this time Singh. Thank you for your answers. I believe you answered truthfully. Thank you. I may send someone over to examine your paperwork at a later date, if you don't mind."

Thomas asks Singh, "I suppose you wouldn't mind if I just have a look around here. Most of the stuff will just be 'Greek' to me. If I have any questions, I'm sure you can answer them sir." Thomas walks away with a different insight then he thought he would have about this fellow. It appears that this man is *innocent*!

So who was the man introduced as Singh at the meeting last night? And, why would they do that. Probably because they knew they wouldn't be able to get the 'real' Singh to cooperate.

"Man, that guy Dorland is as conniving as they come..."
he says to himself in a low whisper. And then he thinks to himself, he's running out of time. Oh! and one more thing Singh mentioned a company, Johnson & Dorkin ... could that be a Dorkin brothers company and that's what ties them into the Ring?"

I could start a whole 'nother career just investigating Transit and it seems like that's what I've been doing most of the time on this case anyway.

Chapter 18
The Bug

[*As Thomas is about to turn up the block, he sits waiting at the light. Just then, a fellow moving a delivery flat-bed full of packages loses it on a large bump and it goes crashing into the passenger side front panel of the car.*]

TaskForce HQ

As he checks into the building, he calls up one of the mechanics and explains what happened. He is informed that they'll take a look and replace the panel for him.

"Good Morning Peters, your not gonna love what just happened to me on the way in. I'm sitting at a light and ..."

"**Not now Thomas!** Seems Mayor Bertrand will have a press conference in about 10 minutes to announce that they have arrested a suspect who they believe is **THE LONE RIDER!**" They'll be a live feed on your computer, so you can watch it at your desk."

"What??? And just who might that be, I wonder?"

Thomas can not believe what is about to happen ...
RING! RRING! Just then the phone rings.
"Banner, This is O'Reilly over in the bay, just wanted to let you know that we just found a tracking device hidden in your car!"
"Are you kidding me?"
"Listen Banner, one of my mechanics was killing time and went to grab the owners manual from the glove compart and spotted the device."
"Is there any thing you can tell me about the device?"
"Nothing too sophisticated. It just emits a tracking beam that another device can pick up—probably has a limited range to do it in. Pretty standard fare I'm told."
"Thanks again O'Reilly ... I got to run."
Thomas thinks to himself, I had a sort of feeling like someone was following me lately. Now who the heck could have ... Slinger that son-of ... I'll bet it was him. Wait until I get my hands on that guy!

Chapter 19
The Capture

Transit

Thomas gets back to his desk just in the nick-of-time, to hear on his computer ...

We interrupt our regularly scheduled programming to bring you the following Press Conference by Mayor Betrand announcing the capture of THE LONE RIDER!

"Good Morning Ladies and Gentlemen. Um ... I am more than happy to announce as of today, that after a long and through investigation between all the Agencies and Departments involved in THE LONE RIDER case, Um ... We have a **suspect** *in custody!*

I particularly wish to single-out a Detective, Um ... who has been instrumental in bring this suspect in, our own Detective Kip Slinger. Additionally I wish to thank the Governor, The Feds, all the local Municipalities involved and especially Transit.

Um ... ummm ... I think the City can rest a little easier now that we discovered who this suspect is. Please direct ummm ... any questions to Detective Slinger's boss, Inspector Jawatson."

"I also have a statement to give to ... Um ... all of you and then both Detective Slinger or I will answer as many questions as we can.—Yesterday, at approximately 4 P.M., A patrol car was involved in high speed pursuit. Detective Slinger was nearby and also gave chase. The suspect eventually had to flee on foot, near the Transit building by the Waterfront. When the Detective confronted the suspect, the suspect had no choice but to surrender. At that time Detective Slinger placed one ... Ummm ..."

James Arrondi,

—that last name is spelled **A R R O N D I**, into custody and pending further investigation, we will assess the total number of charges that will be filed against him," Jawatson said.

"At this time, we believe that *James Arrondi* allegedly acted alone and once certain facts are brought to light that we are sure, that this Um ... wraps up the investigation into THE LONE RIDER case."I would like to bring up to the podium Detective Slinger."

"Thank you Inspector Jawatson." Slinger steps up to the speakers.

"The suspect in custody is a white male approximately 58 years of age 5' 7'' tall with a medium build. he has dirty brown long hair and 2 tattoo's. A small picture of his three kids (in black and white) on his left shoulder and 1 color one, on his left forearm."Slinger says that photo's of the tattoo's will be available sometime after the news conferrence.

"James Arthur Arrondi, was a former Employee of the Developed Technologies Department of Transit, where he basically worked in the bullpen. A jack-of-all-trades in the department. He has no criminal record and his driving record is clean. It is unclear at this time, if he has ever been in the military."

Jawatson indicates that Slinger and himself will now take questions from the press. "Just keep in mind fellows that we can only release the most very basic of information at this time ..."

"Detective, can you tell us if Arrondi put up any resistance before his capture?"
"Yes, he did and he has some bruises to show for it."
" A follow-up if I may?
Was he carrying a weapon of any kind?"
"No. but there was a weapon in his vehicle, we are attempting to find out if he has a license for it "

"What did he say to you when you captured him"
"I'm innocent!"

"When can we talk to him, Jawatson?"
"Listen, we need some time on this one ..."

"Was he caught red-handed —Inspector?"
"At this time, I am not at liberty to discuss those details with you. From time-to-time we will release some ... ummm ... some statements and documents"

"Detective Slinger my name is Christopher Drake with the Daily Flush—I understand that Special Agents from the TaskForce worked on this case since the very beginning —did they or you share any information to aide in capturing the suspect?

"Christopher Drake, At this time I am not at liberty to discuss those details of the case with you. except to say that we always have cooperation between the various Dements, in any particular Investigation."

"Where is he being held?"

"He has been processed through Central Booking and resides now in an undisclosed location for his own protection. He is also under an around-the-clock suicide prevention watch."

"Johnathon Cliff from Pict2Pix.com—What does he need protection from? Are you trying to hide something?"

"Cliff, We have nothing to hide. At some later date there will be another news conference, Umm ... where we will present Mr. Arrondi to the media. As for the moment, he is at an undisclosed location because there have been several threats against his life. We don't want this situation to get out of hand, where we have a lynch-mob mentality around here."

"OK folks, we're going to have to wrap things up here, Yes, Mr. Drake you have the last one this time."
"We are grateful that Detective Slinger has taken the alleged LONE RIDER off the streets and given the fact that this same Detective's arrest record is far from stellar. Should we expect a follow-up lawsuit from the defendant because of his excessive use of force."
"And, that ends this press conference. Thank you Ladies and Gentlemen of the Press.

Peters runs in and says to Thomas:

"Those S.O.B.'s just blindsided us! I can't believe that they're gonna try and get away with this Shit! said Peters

"WHO THE HELL IS JAMES ARRONDI???"

Thomas replies that "I interviewed him awhile back and he is on my suspect list, but nowhere near the top. He's a retired former employee from Transit."

"So HOW COME we didn't capture him ourselves?"

"Sir, I have a hunch that this arrest was just for show or to throw us off the trail. Somethings just not right with this arrest. There was no mention at all about any of the evidence during the press conference." Thomas also mentioned that ...

"The only actual questions during that press shindig that weren't softballs, were from Drake and you know it." Thomas continues talking, sitting down now. "This had all the grand making of a dog-and-pony show. They'll let this Arrondi guy go shortly."

"I'm sure this has been kicked upstairs now, it's out of my hands Thomas so, just don't do anything stupid. And stay away from Slinger—UNDERSTOOD!"

Thomas thinks to himself. I'm sure it's a frame job. I going to go down to Slinger's office and confront that bastard about that thing in my car. And I going to see if I can find out anything more about this big arrest.

Just then, Drake calls ... "Give me a minute. Nice job on those guys by the way." Thomas says ..."Anyhow, what can you tell me about this situation and what do you honestly think about it."

"Thom listen, this press thing was just thrown together on short notice, there was no time to let you know. *I just had to go with the flow*. It seems a little unusual so, I'm going to see if I can uncover anything else about it. Of course, as far as my paper is concerned, tomorrows headline will be splattered on page one:

"LONE RIDER STOPPED *BEFORE* HE GETS STARTED!
Lead story written by yours truly."

"Yeah Drake, the whole thing stinks. Soon as this guy heals a little bit, they'll parade Arrondi around and he'll protest his innocents. In the meantime they will have kept the wolfs-at-bay, with the hope that they will find the real LONE RIDER." Thomas said with disgust.

"Apparently, one of my colleagues at the paper found out that they were under such intense pressure to find a suspect that just to shut-up the Governor and the Mayor's crew, they seemed to have 'gathered up the usual suspects' and then selected Arrondi."

"Any idea where they might be holding him?"

"That Thom, is the million-dollar question. Of course. I'll have my sources looking into it, but it's like looking for some sort of a needle-in-a-haystack. If I were you, I think I'd go and ask Slinger himself."

Chapter 20
The Answer?

Police Headquarters

Thomas shows up looking for Slinger and is given the runaround.

"He's in his office, Ahhhh ... No, No, he's just stepped out. No, he's on a case and won't be around for a couple of days." The front desk Sargent is obviously making stuff up.

Thomas finally says to him "Look you tell him, I'm coming after him and I will find him ..."

Thomas is about to head back to to the office, when he gets another call from Drake.

"Thom listen, I have it on good authority that Slinger is hiding the suspect upstairs at ClubWINK, that Gentlemen's Club over in Midtown."

[*ClubWINK is a known risqué business, catering to an upscale clientele that usually revolves right around the shader side of life. Supposedly, all sorts of illegal activities go on there all the time. The problem ... is that they employ State-of-the-Art electronic warning systems and their working girls are well schooled in how to behave, so that they operate just inside of what's legal. There have been many attempts to shut-down the place, all to no avail. As it turns out ... Slinger works there after hours, as part of the Security Force there.*]

"Are you sure Christopher?" Thomas asks?

"Slinger will be holding court there tonight. He and James Arrondi are probably going to be there some time after eleven!"

"Thanks Christopher, maybe I can get to the bottom of this thing after all. Just out of curiosity, how did you find out?"

"Well, Headi Mascara, one of the exotic dancers over there got busted and was looking to make a deal. She was smart enough to know that giving up this information would help her case."

"You know Christopher, you should have come to work for the TaskForce."

"As you already know, you guys don't make nearly enough

money. You don't get any of the glory, like we do. And, our boss doesn't have to wear a badge, to kick our butts Thom!"

"Yeah, but lousy pay and a short life span surely make up for that Christopher."

"You're right Thomas! I may have to reconsider ..."

TaskForce HQ

Thomas has gone back to the office to check-in and see if anything else has happened today. Peters comes into his office and asks "What do you have for me Banner, any update on that arrest?" Thomas looks straight at him and says "I think I have some information that might straighten out the whole thing, but maybe, they may have really caught the guy. Who knows?"

Peters looks at him and figures that's just Banner's way of telling him to back-off a little bit, so he turns around and leaves.

Thomas picks up the phone "Honey, I'm definitely going to be home late again ..." Christine says on the phone ...

"Thomas you ... said that you were going to stop this—you promised me that you were going to stop doing that for these last couple of months..."

"Yeah! ... I know, but there's this thing I just have to check in about and it might be the answer ... I ..."
Thomas' voice trails off. He knows he's said this to Christine hundreds of times and that he probably will have to say this to her a few more times, before he puts in his papers.

"Hon, I don't have much longer to go and you know I need to see this case to the end. I promise, I'll make all of this up to you and the guys when I retire. We're going to go great places and do great things, I promise you and the boys ... I swear."
Thomas catches up with tons of paperwork at the office. For him, the hours seem to drag by. One of the things that has eaten up a lot of his time in the last couple of weeks, is the fact that cases that he passed to others, still needed his help.

He has had to spend his time in countless courtrooms testifying about his knowledge of certain cases. Some of them have gone on far longer then he expected. Anyway, Thomas looks up...

The clock has hit 9:30, so he goes on his way to ClubWINK!

Chapter 21
The WINK!

ClubWINK

Thomas walks in and scopes the place out. It seems that they have way more security personnel than they should have a need for. He looks around towards the bar and..

(THE MUSIC IS BOOMING!!!)

WAIT A MINUTE ...!

What's this? Who is sitting by the bar, but Christopher Drake. Thomas walks up to the bar and Christopher says ...
 "Hello fellow. Can I buy you a drink?"
 "Sure, why not? Make that a Scotch and soda." Thomas is not happy about this situation. If any trouble breaks out, he doesn't want Christopher getting hurt. By the way, Drake says he's been here for sometime and there's no sign of Arrondi.

[*Christopher Drake is a 50+ heavyset, out of shape, beat reporter. He is single and has no relatives. For him, the job is his life. He has been a reporter for The Daily Flush for almost seventeen years. He is also a Vietnam Veteran that served two tours and would have served more, if he didn't blow out his knee, escaping his captors.*]

 Just for your information." Christopher says "Slinger is in the back, behind that door, where that big beefy bouncer has been sitting." Then Christopher whispers in his ear ...
 "I think you should stay here awhile before you go into that room. Finish your drink. I mean relax. Look, have you ever seen a more beautiful group of half-naked women dancing around in your entire life. I mean that's what brings me here."
 "So you've been here *before* Christopher."
 "No Thomas, not EVER!"
 "And you just happened to pick T-O-N-I-G-H-T to check the place out. I never cease to be amazed by you sometimes."
 "Everybody's got to have a hobby, mine is chasing down a story

when it's alive and that **'Buzz'** is going on. At that moment, I feel more alive then, I have ever felt. It's almost like being back in the War. I mean, it was an absolutely terrible, scary time. More than you could ever imagine, but on occasion it was just crazy!"

"Well listen Christopher, if any shit goes down, you get the hell out of here, as fast as you can. And, DON'T COME BACK!"

"Look Thomas, if you're thinking of pulling a stunt—you're really out-manned and out-gunned here. You better call for back-up, if you think you're going to go in there alone."

Christopher continues "I know ... I know Slinger's department is probably pulling a fast one, but you guys should just file some paperwork protest from one Big-Shot mucky-muck to the other. Besides, they're probably going to shut this place down sooner or later. I'm thinking sooner, although, some of these women are just..."

"Keep it in your pants Christopher, besides, I here for a far different reason. Somebody bugged my cars and I'm pretty sure that, that S.O.B Slinger, was the one who did it! So, I'm going to go in there and tear him a new A-H___!"

Thomas then turns rapidly away from Christopher and heads towards the place where he has seen Slinger come in and out of.

"Thomas NO! ... Wait ... I was the One ..." Christopher says, but Thomas does not hear, he is moving fast and is too far away.

On the way to his destination, a beautiful blonde who was about to go on stage passes right by Thomas. She is so stunning that he just had to turn and look at her. She turns to him and opens her robe and WINKS! She is completely *NAKED* under that robe. Thomas turns back and two Security guys grab his arms to prevent him from going in.

"And, just where do you think you're headed?"one of them says to him.

Tell Slinger, Special Agent Banner's here to see him." His voice is now raised "Tell him he's got two minutes to let me in or I'll make such a terrible scene, it'll scare away all two of his customers. Tell him..." Just then Slinger appears, as one of the security guys punches Thomas in the gut. Slinger is NOT happy.

UGH!
Thomas falls to his knees.

They drag him into the room and throw him on a chair. Slinger says
"Fellas, that wasn't necessary. It might get to that, but you were
a little too hasty about it. Next time, wait for my signal."

"So what's your problem Banner, You're just pissed that we
caught the suspect and you guys didn't. I mean this is a nice place,
you could have had a few drinks, maybe I'd throw you a free lap
dance from one of the girls or something ... Why'd you have to go
and get me angry?"

"I told you, we weren't finished Slinger and that stunt you
pulled. Do you really think I wouldn't find out?"
"What the Hell are you talking about? What stunt? We just found
James Arrondi because of good detective work"
"You know very well that's not what I'm talking about. I'm
talking about the Goddamn **bugs you planted** in my cars!" Thomas
is shouting now."
"Keep your voice down Banner. First-off, I don't know what the
heck your talking about. I never planted a bug in your car! Now,
Slinger is angry and is in Thomas' face and pointing at him.

"YOU'RE FULL OF CRAP, SLINGER!"

Slinger nods at one of the men and he hits Thomas so hard across
the face that he falls off the chair.
WHAM!

They pick him back up and put him back in the chair.
***"I told you to keep QUIET! Nobody calls me a liar and gets
away with it. And, just for the record, I didn't plant those damm
bugs..."***

Christopher was standing near the door, listening to everything.
(Nobody was outside, since the guards were all inside the room.)
He knew that his friend was now in trouble and he was going to
do anything he could to help.
BOOM!

A moment or two after Thomas hit the floor, Christopher rushed the door and knocked it open. Thomas then took advantage of the momentary distraction and turned around and knocked out the guy who had hit him in the face!

The other guard pulled out a gun and Christopher hit him full-on with a chair, knocking him down and out.
CRASH!

Meanwhile Slinger ran towards the door where Thomas got ahold of him and the next thing you know both of them are on the ground, fists flying, legs kicking and the two of them rolling all around the room.

Just then the rest of the Security force rushes into the room where Christopher is attempting to hold them off with another chair. He turns back to Thomas and says ...

"THOMAS LISTEN TO ME! Slinger had nothing to do with those bugs. *I had them planted!* I did it so I might get a scope for the investigation and have it printed in The Daily Flush! I was ...

POP! POP!
The Security guard that Christopher hit with the chair, woke up and pulled out his gun, and shoots him!

Christopher drops to the ground clutching his chest and Thomas runs over to him and cradles him in his arms.
    "Hey ... not to bad for an old guy, Huh?"
    "Not bad at all Chris, you did great!"
    "You called me Chris! In all ... the years I've ... known you ...
—you never called ... me that."

"YOU earned it today buddy." Thomas can feel the life draining out of him. "Somebody call an Ambulance, **NOW!**"

Slinger nods to one of the Security guards—who runs to make the phone call. Slinger in the meantime has placed the guard who did the shooting under arrest.

    "You know what's really ... pissing me off Thomas (cough) I ... didn't get to use any of those skills that I learned during the (cough)War years—all that self-defense (cough)(cough) down the drain right?"

"Hey (cough) Thomas ... I ... just ... got to tell you ... I got that **'Buzz'** ... for the last time. And, you ... (cough) called me Chris. I guess (cough)(cough) this was (cough) all worth (cough) it...!"

Christopher Drake has died in Thomas' arms.

Slinger bends down on one knee near the two of them and says ...
" I just want to say I'm sorry about this. I told you I didn't ..."
"Just let it go Slinger. Get everyone out of here and let me have some time with him."
"Sure Banner, whatever you want."

In about two minutes, the ambulance arrives and the paramedics did everything they could to revive him. They got his heart to start again TWICE, but they could never sustain it. Christopher died on the way to the Hospital. Thomas was in the Ambulance when he passed away. Later Thomas heads to the office, on a mission!

TaskForce HQ
Thomas walks into the office, turns on the lights and his computer. He then proceeds to write the 'story' of what happened this night at the ClubWink. After he had written four or five pages, he prints it and signs it *Christopher Drake!* Thomas then throws it into a manilla envelope and seals it.

The Daily Flush
[*Thomas then gets into his car and proceeds to The Daily Flush, where he drops off the story into a box outside the Editors room. He thinks he got it there just in time to make the morning edition.*]

Thomas figures that, that was the least he could do for his buddy. At least, his last story will get published. Somehow this seemed to make Thomas feel just a little bit better.

He thought to himself—and all this time, I was convinced that Slinger had planted those bugs—but it was Chris ... Imagine that.

Chapter 22
The Headline!

TaskForce HQ

Thomas didn't go home last night. He didn't want to disturb his family and he knew he wouldn't get any sleep anyway. So he stayed at his desk, just reminiscing about all the funny stuff that had happened between him and Christopher over the years.

He thought about how much they had helped each other over the years too.

And he waited ...

He thought about the fact that Christopher had shown up at that bar because, he thought that Thomas would need some back-up.

And he waited ...

He thought about the fact that there was less than five weeks left in his investigation.

And he waited ... and waited ...

FINALLY, he ran downstairs, knowing that the latest edition of The Daily Flush had just hit the streets!

Sure enough, when he picked the paper up in his hands, he was surprised to see that the Editor hadn't changed a thing. That he had published the headline just as Thomas had written it. It seemed a fitting tribute to a totally professional guy and a good friend ...

And, inside on page one, was the story just as Thomas had written it too. They hadn't changed anything on that either! He was almost beside himself, with a sense of great relief. (Thomas had searched Christopher's coat on the night he died and found his notes on the beginning of the story. The rest concerned an eyewitness account from him—but written as if it was Christopher.

The Daily Flush

REPORTER KILLED IN THE 'WINK' OF AN EYE!

As reported by Christopher Drake

Yesterday, an altercation took place inside a Gentlemen's Club called ClubWINK. I went there looking to see if I could find out any more information about the suspect they had sequestered away in THE LONE RIDER case. I had received a tip that the Detective involved in the arrest would be there and I had hoped to get an interview with him.

I intended to ask a number of questions about the suspect and to try and ascertain the whereabouts, of one James Arrondi.

You, the public, are anxious to know the full story and we at this newspaper are dedicated to getting to the bottom of this.

Remember, that it was this paper that originally doubled the reward money, for information leading the arrest and capture of a suspect. That reward money eventually climbed to **Fifty Thousand Dollars!**

And, we intend to get to the bottom of this, if it takes our last breath ...

EDITORS NOTE: *It is our sad duty to inform you the Reader that, Christopher Drake was shot and killed in the line of duty as he rushed in during a violent altercation, and saved the life of a Special Agent.*

We at the paper, his family and his friends will miss his wit, his wisdom, and his tenacity as a reporter. He chose to put himself in harms way, to do his job. Our Readers will miss his writing.

We have created a Journalism Award in Christopher's name.

Chapter 23
The Wake

Cemetery

Thomas went to the wake and now, to the burial of his friend, Christopher Drake. A number of VIP's attended including the Editor of Christopher's newspaper.

Thomas couldn't help, but reflect on the fact that there was no 21 gun salute, no televised ceremony, no thousands of fellow workers lining the route, like his partner had when he died.

Just a handful of friends and one or two beat reporters.

In an unusual move, the Editor of the newspaper had asked Thomas to say a few words at the gravesite. Thomas was honored to do so.

"To Christopher's friends and those in attendance today, and especially his loyal readers. A precious voice has been lost and yet while Chris was here, he made a tremendous difference."

Thomas paused and took a deep breath.
"If you were fortunate enough to meet him, you realized that he had a real fire in his belly, an unending look for the truth and a pain that, that truth sometimes revealed to him AND us."

Again, Thomas tried to find the right words ...
"More times then he liked to admit, he was most disappointed in the corruption, indecency and the complacency. He was most satisfied I think, when the web of deceit was exposed and the truth was revealed for all to see. And hopefully that it spurred a resolution or a resurrection for those involved ..."

—Everyone there was touched by his eloquent use of words.

Of course, the next day The Daily Flush called for the murderer to be **sentenced to death!**

Chapter 24
The Beginning.

[In the ensuing investigation, the ClubWINK was shut down due to a number of violations, including weapons and drug charges.

Detective Slinger was issued a summons and was being informally investigated by his Internal Affairs Department, he has been given a desk job. (Since he was off-duty at the time of the incident, no formal charges were brought forward.)

The Security Guard responsible for killing Christopher Drake, a, Clinton DeFontaine, was arrested and booked on a charge of murder. He is currently detained in a men's correctional facility.]

TaskForce HQ
Thomas puts in a call to Detective Slinger.

"Slinger, this is Banner, I was wondering if you would like to meet."

"Look, I don't think we have anything to talk about. I said all I needed to say at the ClubWINK. Because of you, I lost my gig there, I'm being investigated here and I've been given a desk job." Slinger sounds really pissed!

I just found out that the Editor of The Flush thinks I should be prosecuted, as an accessary to the murder. Now, I need to get a high priced lawyer—and who's gonna pay for that? You?"

"I just wanted to make a deal with you, about Arrondi."

"No freakin' way Banner."

"Well, it was worth a shot. Maybe, this is the way that you want to end your career. Remember, public opinion is a powerful thing. If that Editor decides to stir up the pot—you may need all the help you can get your hands on.

Slinger thinks about what Banner has said and then says:

"Ok, where do you want to meet?"

"How about at the Horse-White Tavern right down around the Waterfront?"

"Yeah, that will do, say around 2 P.M.?"

"Yeah Slinger, just make sure you show up!"

Thomas is really surprised that Slinger didn't need to be persuaded by anything else, but he is grateful for the meeting.

Thomas reflects on the fact that while all this was going on, he didn't have a chance to follow-up on an investigation into all those who attended that meeting back at ANVIL2.

And he needs to find out who was introduced as R. Singh at that meeting and he needs to check out the brothers Dorkin. And, after he talks with Slinger, he wants to speak with Jawatson. He also needs to also go and visit Beatty Morgenstern and Matt Dorland. *And everything takes so much time ...*

Thomas also takes out the sheet of paper with the list that he unfortunately has to update again:

Deceased

Joseph Sorelo
Scanner Simmons
Ronald Rimsum
(& 2 men and a woman)
Carlos Allcus
Christopher Drake

Horse-White tavern

Thomas arrives early and sits at the bar waiting for Slinger.
Slinger walks in about ten minutes later and they proceed to get a table.

Thomas says to Slinger "So, how's it going?"

"Shitty, *really shitty!*"

"I'll get straight to the point. I want to talk to James Arrondi in person. I want you to arrange it."

"Listen Banner, I can arrange it, but I'm going to have insist that I'm there too, or it's no deal."

"Listen Slinger, I don't think you're in any position to dictate the terms. I want five full minutes with him alone—you can wait outside, if you like." Thomas knows he's going to have to agree.

"So, tell me if I'm wrong. This is how I see it. You guys were getting desperate and you were under a lot of pressure to produce a suspect. So somehow you picked Arrondi, how that happened I'm not exactly sure? maybe you or someone in your department even planted some evidence? Or maybe you had him on some other charge and decided he'd make the perfect *patsy*? Then, probably at the end of this week you're going to have to let him go for lack of evidence etc. Isn't that just about the way it went."

"You're absolutely right Banner!"

Then after a long pause Slinger says *"Except for a few things*. First of all, he's the real deal. Secondly, we didn't have to plant a damm thing. Thirdly, he is not going to be released—*he's going to be convicted!*

Thomas can't believe what he's hearing. *Why would Slinger stick to that story?* He's got to know something I don't ...

"So what evidence do you have? And convict him of what? *No crime has been committed—if there's no victim!"*
Thomas continues "Unless you intend to let him go and then he commits the murder and then you arrest him! But that would mean that you are aiding and abetting a criminal. So you see Slinger, the story you're telling just doesn't make any sense."

"OK, I'll spell it out for you Banner. After a very, very through investigation, we belive he was responsible for those three murders that took place at Ronald Rimsums' house. We also believe he tortured and killed Rimsum later on.

[*When James was pursued and then captured—they found the murder weapon in his car. Ballistics tests confirmed this.*]

Slinger is very animated now "So we have him for murder one, we have the murder weapon and we have the motive."

"What motive, for a bunch of Transit doodads!?"

"No Banner, those people (Rimsum and the others) were all killed for want of a ... Collectible ClickCard."

He got Banner's attention now ...

"When we interrogated Arrondi he knew we had him, but he wouldn't talk. He clammed up and nothing we did was going to change his mind. Then we got a phone call at the precinct, from someone who said that "She would *kill* Arrondi if he decided to talk. She would kill him in the precinct, in the courthouse or in prison. There was nowhere that her money or her reach could not get her." She certainly sounded like she meant it.

"Then she said something interesting ... we could *make a deal.*
If we shifted away from the murders and focused on James being the suspect—THE LONE RIDER, then she would provide to us two pieces of evidence. One, she would send us now and the other would be provided two weeks after we held a Press Conference naming him as the suspect."

Faced with the prospect of losing our suspects life, we made the deal and moved him to an undisclosed location."

"So, what was the evidence she provided, Slinger?"

"She provided dates and bank accounts that showed that large sums of money had shown up in several of his accounts that he can't possibly explain. Money, it was stated that was his share of the selling of that collectible ClickCard. The one that he managed to take from Rimsum, after he tortured him!
The second piece of information that she provided to us was the location of a trapdoor that was inside Arrondi apartment, that we managed to miss, when we went through his place.

And, just like she said, inside that trapdoor was the computer, the printer, flash drives and CD's and external hard drives.

She said "They would, if dusted for fingerprints, prove that this equipment was Arrondi's. And, that there were discarded printouts of the original letter from 'The Lone Rider' along with the actual computer file the letter was composed on."

Thomas was in shock! *This was in no way how he pictured any of this unfolding.* But who was this woman who had provided all of this information?

"Do you have any idea who this woman was, Slinger?"

"NO! Not a clue, and everything she sent was wiped clean. Also her voice was mechanically altered, like she was talking through some kind of modified voicebox. So, I have no idea how old she is or what she looked like."

"Did she say anything unusual? Or do anything that you thought was strange?"

"The only thing I noticed was that she seemed to be way overly concerned with how Arrondi was being treated. Was he hurt? Was he being treated alright?" Kind of odd, I'm thinking?

"By the way, the other thing was that none of the packages sent, were by mail, they were actually just randomly dropped off at the office or left outside. We never even noticed who delivered them and we even staked our own place out. *Must have been an inside job!* Apparently, she really could have reached him in here.

"Slinger there's just two more things I need to ask you and then I'll see what I can do about your situation. Now that I have had an interaction with the Editor, I'll see if I can get him to take it easy on you. I'm not promising anything, but you never know what can happen."

"Thanks Banner, now what else do you need to know?"

"What can you tell me about Arrondi. How did he come to know that Rimsum and those others were involved with the ClickCard? And, when can I get to meet him?"

"The reason he knew about Rimsum and those others was that he had someone on the inside—Charyse Higgins."

Slinger went on to say that "He was involved with her and that she was the widow of a Transit employee. Arrondi said that she was the common law wife of a fellow named Arthur Askins. He died tragically and she had a lot of mouths to feed. There was some big lawsuit pending, but she hadn't seen any money.

—Anyhow, just before he died, Askins had told her that he had come into information about something really fantastic! Something that was going to change them and their kids lives ... Just before he died, he had told her how to get ahold of it. How she could get her hands on something worth Millions!"

"So when can I see him?"

"Give me 24 hours and I'll take you to him."

"OK Slinger, but you better not try to pull anything ..."

Thomas looked at him and knew that he wasn't going to fool around this time.

"So, Arrondi supposedly got greedy and killed all those people for the Card?" Thomas was amazed and he thought to himself.

—How small a world it really is.

Chapter 25
The Target?

[Slinger and Thomas head out to a small Safe House where James Arrondi is being held.]

Safe House

As they pull up to the front of the house, there is a plainclothes Detective sitting outside the door and Thomas fully expects to find another inside the house with the suspect.

Slinger directs the two Detectives to take some time-off, get a cup of coffee or something and come back, in about a half-hour. "There you go Banner, I've kept my end of this bargain. "You've got about 5 minutes and I'll be waiting right outside."

James Arrondi is surprised to see Special Agent Thomas Banner again. He's wondering what the heck does this guy want with me now?

"James, I just want to ask you a few questions and you'd better be straight with me, as far as your answers."

"Look Banner, I've already answered a million questions so, unless you think you can get me outta here and can make these charges against me disappear ..."

"Listen James, I just want to know if you have any clue as to who this woman was who called and threatened your life? WHACK!

James suddenly hits Thomas across the face and tries to get past him. Thomas as he is falling, reaches out and grabs James leg and trips him up and jumps on top of him— cuffing him.

Thomas drags him to the bed and makes him sit there. Wiping away the blood from his lip with a handkerchief, Thomas says, "that was a pretty stupid thing to do ..." Banner then throws the cuffs on him.

Just then Slinger swings open the door to see what has happened. "Are you OK Banner?"

"Yeah, I'm fine, but if James doesn't give me the answers I'm looking for ... I'm not so sure that he'll be alright."

Slinger says to James "You don't want to piss this guy off—trust me!" Slinger goes back outside.

"Look Banner, I'm being set-up for this whole thing. I'm innocent, I swear!!!"

"One more time, do you know who that woman was?"

"No, but I could probably take a guess."

"So, who is she James?"

"Back in the day, I knew her as Lorraine Hicks, but I hear she goes by another name now. I believe her name is ... Beatty ... Beatty Morgenstern!!!

*"Beatty Morgenstern? Are you **sure** James!?"*

"As you probably know Banner, I was in the service. There was a place we used ..."

"Yeah, I think I know the rest of the story now. You used to go to this place when you and the boys got into town. And, there was this young women ... Lorraine you said, that was very popular with all of them. And you and her got really cozy with one another and started to see each other a lot.'

"Yeah, that's it, but it was me who talked her out of working there anymore." He then says ...

"Why, I'd even asked her to marry me!"

Thomas was amazed at what he was hearing.

"—There was this other guy there, a guy named Matt, who worked there and was seeing her. Well, he wasn't to happy that I took her away from him. He had lots a dough, but his family didn't want him involved in any sort of illegal stuff. I guess they put pressure on him to stop working there and go legit, and he eventually did, I heard."

"By any chance are you talking about a guy named Matt Dorland?"

"How did you know that Banner?"

"*Just a lucky guess!* And, if she is the one that provided that information to Slinger about you, than *Dorland is the guy framing* you. And if he's framing you, then that evidence provided is really his. Are you with me so far James?"

"Yeah, that's what I've been saying—I've been framed!"

"Only one problem with your story. Dorland might be clever,

dishonest, shrewd and nasty, but he'd never resort to murder. And, since you were caught with the murder weapon, how do you explain that?"

"I can't say, if I do he'll kill me."

"*Who'll kill you?* Listen, we don't have any more time. Slinger is going to come in here, at any moment and I'm going to have to leave. Do you understand me, James?"

"I was ... was returning ... the gun to ... *Paul Dorkins!*"

James then continued his story.

"Years ago, I used to do some freelance stuff on the side, for the Dorkins. He called me and said he needed to borrow my car 'cause his was in the shop. he told me I could come by the next day, to pick up the car at his shop."

I did and then I got a call from him on my cell, "he said that he had left a 'stunt' pistol in the car from an independent movie he was helping to finance. He asked if I could bring the gun back to his shop." James explained that before he gave it back to him, he picked it up and pretended to aim and shoot it a couple of times."

James now knows, what a *dumb* thing that was to do ...

"I HAD NO IDEA, IT WAS A REAL GUN! That's where my fingerprints came from. My guess is that he had wiped the gun prior to my handling it. How he would have know, that I would pick it up, I have no idea. Or, maybe he just got Lucky."
Thomas just has a gut feeling that James is telling the truth.

"Go on James, continue."

"The next thing I know is that I'm pursued and then I'm arrested man, and everything else that has happened since then, has been UNREAL!"

Just then Slinger opened the door and said that "time was up, Banner." He looked at James still handcuffed, sitting on the bed, "you can remove those now ... Thomas."

"Yeah, I will." he looks directly at James, "but if I find out that anything you told me was untrue then, I'm going to come back here and finish that little bit of business that we started."
Thomas meant what he said ... then he bends over and whispers

"James, there's just one more thing. IF everything you said is true ... *how do you explain* all that money, in all those bank accounts, that are in your name?"

"That's just it—I can't. Unless, they were looking to get rid of me and then have someone take my place ... I don't know ... I have no clue ... It's certainly NOT my money!"

Thomas looks at him and says ...

"Maybe someone was going to replace you, but probably not in person, but take your place *electronically!* I would think they would Internet the money to some off-shore account, if you are out of the picture. Which means they were planning to get rid of you in prison, *or sooner.* But right now it's just a theory I have."

Slinger says "I hope you found out what you needed and that you won't forget me Thomas. These guys watching James stuck their necks out pretty far for me today, so don't let me down."

"After what I found out now, I'll get right on it as soon as I get back to the office Slinger."

James gave some thought as to what Thomas had said to him and started to panic and wants to change his story ...

"Hey BANNER! I did *lie* to you about one thing. Paul never told me to come by the next day—he took my car, 'cause I owed him money from a gambling debt. I just went back there and stole it back from him. I really did get that cell-phone call, you can check."

"I will James, I will ..."

Chapter 26
The Respect

TaskForce HQ

Thomas gets in very early today and places a call to the Editor of The Daily Flush, Mel Oats. He knows that newspaper men are very early risers.

[Mr. Oats has been the Editor of The Daily Flush for the last 15 years or so. A thin man with white hair who is approaching his 82nd year. He has edited stories of every kind. He has seen leaders large and small, come and go. Some of them by his own hand. He is both the most feared and just about the most respected man in the newspaper business today.

If his paper endorses you, than you are a shoe-in to win/get whatever. If his paper targets you, it is said that it would take, an act of God or someone almost as high up, like Oats himself, to change it. It has only happened twice in ten years.]

"Mr. Oats this is Special Agent Thomas Banner, Sir."

"What's on your mind Thomas."

"Sir, I'm sorry to trouble you sir. You see sir, I have a bit of a problem and I need your Assistance ..."

"Stop calling me Sir. You can call me Mel, if you like. You are asking for *my help*, this is most unusual!"

"I know, I know sir, but I need ... your publication ... to back-off of Detective Slinger for just a little bit, that's all ..."

"Thomas you're asking me to shun my duty to 'expose' this scoundrel and all those in this great City, who do us harm, just on your say so?" This is a typical good cop gone bad story.

"It involves our investigation into THE LONE RIDER case. Detective Slinger has been very instrumental in providing me with information that will allow me to solve the case. If you could just see your way clear to doing this one thing. I know my request is a little unorthodox, but I'm so sure I'm on the right track sir."

"Haven't you been READING my paper son!?"

Mel asks in ernest. *"We've already announced who the main suspect is Thomas."*

"With all due respect sir. If you're half as good of an Editor as I believe you to be, then you know that James Arrondi is not the guy. Why he's **no more guilty than you or I.**"

Thomas decides to gamble and says to Mr Oats:

"Yes Sir, I urge you to DO YOUR CIVIC DUTY and report that the story needs to be revisited or something like that. Heck, you're the Editor, *you'll think of something!"*

There is a really long pause on the other end of the phone ...

"Thomas come to think of it, I do believe that, that story is not really as high profile as I once thought it was. And there are definitely some other stories that need to see the light of day, that I might even consider ... for an example, I think the 64th District is looking to dedicate a very small area in the neighborhood as a bird sanctuary." Oats pauses again for affect.

" In other words, I'll see what I can do Thomas."

"Thank you Sir, I'm much obliged."
"The names Mel ... goodbye Thomas."

Chapter 27
The Ruse

TaskForce HQ

Thomas decides to go on the Internet and see if he can come up with anything unusual about the Dorkin brothers. He goes on a search engine and finds that these fellows had inherited the business from their father, who had done fairly well locally. When they took over the business, they poured money into it, and now the company is global.

In recent years they have turned their attention into financing independent films. Having had some success, it enabled them to start to hobnobbing with the rich and famous. So, apparently they are no strangers to 'red carpet' events and film festivals.

Of course, there is no mention anywhere of any alleged gambling forays ... But so far, James story sounds about right.

Thomas calls their office and is told that the brothers are out of town for the next week, working with a new client who needs their equipment. So much for going to see them.

Thomas' mind now turns towards Beatty Morgenstern. She *never* mentioned James Arrondi to him, when she told him her story. He then places a call to Gail Diaz and asks her if there is anytime when he might be able to talk to her. Diaz gives him her schedule and her home address and suggests that if this is really urgent, that he should talk to her, when she goes to get into her car from the Railroad. She also provides Thomas with Beatty's license plate number and the make and model of her car.

"Did Beatty ever mention a James Arrondi to her"

"Well, for a while he used to call her and they would talk for a fairly long time. Then I guess things got a little awkward, 'cause he used to keep asking her for money."

"Do you know what he needed the money for Gail?"

"Yeah, it was for a gambling debt, on occasion she would ask me to bring a manila envelope to him. It was obvious to me that the envelopes had money, lots of money inside them."

"How often did you bring him money?"

Well Thomas, for awhile it was regular, like clockwork, every two month or so."

"Thanks again Gail, I'll talk to you soon."

Thomas figures that James must have blackmailed Beatty. Poor girl, she was really getting it from both ends. Dorland making her do things at work and James getting money from her. It's like she was being blackmailed *twice* ...

—And still she managed to lead two distinctly separate lives!

Now, as to that gambling thing between James and Paul Dorkin, what was that all about? What kind of gambling are we talking about, Thomas thinks he might have the answer. But first he's going to have to talk to Beatty, later that evening.

And, if James really didn't commit those murders of Rimsum and the others, than who did? Is it possible that Paul or his brother Charlie did? Didn't seem to make sense, but then nothing did on this case.

It was times like these that made Thomas miss his old friend Christopher Drake. I would just have to make one phone call and usually he'd come back with a lead from the streets. Even though his own department had pretty good sources on the street, it just wasn't the same as Christopher's stuff ...

Anyhow, he needed to leave now, if he wanted to get to the Railroad in time to catch Beatty, before she went home.

—Just then Paul Peters, his boss, comes into the room and hands him a sheet of paper and says:

"You're not going to like what this says ... Thomas!"

"What's up Paul?"

"OH MY GOD!"

Thomas looks at it and drops the report on the desk. It seems that James Arrondi has been *killed* trying to escape! Actually, he was killed by a car. The death appears to be an accident ...

"What are Slinger and the big boys Uptown going to do, now

that he's dead." Peters asks.

"Probably, to cover their own asses, they're going to hold another Press Conference to say that there is ***NO LONGER A THREAT*** on September 17, 2011. That since the alleged suspect, had died while in custody, by accident ... that the City and Transit, and especially the Public could relax. And that there would be no reward payed out." Thomas said in speculation.

"Of course, nothing could be further from the truth ..."

Well, he was still going to head over to the Railroad since Beatty was on the train and would not have heard about Arrondi's death.

But before he goes, he pulls out that piece of paper and once again and adds a name to it. Thomas still can't get over the fact that since he started the investigation of THE LONE RIDER case there have been at least 9 deaths!

He hopes that that's the last time he has to take out this list.

Deceased

Joseph Sorelo
Scanner Simmons
Ronald Rimsum
(& 2 men and a woman)
Carlos Allcus
Christopher Drake
James Arrondi

Thomas figures that for as long as he's been with the TaskForce, that's close to seventy-five and maybe it's closer to eighty people who have been killed. And that's not counting those who died in the line of duty, to which he would need to add another fifteen names. So, I have to balance all of those who are gone, with the thousands that we have put away, where they can no longer be a threat of any kind to society. And, then there are the untold thousands of cases that prevented the loss of life, and property.

Chapter 28
The Chance

RailRoad station

Thomas got there just about three minutes early. Sure enough, the train pulled in, just on time. He was parked right across from her car and waited for her a couple of minutes before she arrived. As she was attempting to get into her car, Thomas stepped out of his. As he got closer, he whispered:

"Beatty, it's Banner, I was wondering if I could talk to you for a couple of minutes?"

"This really isn't a good time Thomas. My kid's sick and I need to go home. Why don't you call me tomorrow and we can set up a time ..."

"Beatty I didn't drive all the way out here ... I need to talk to you *now*! We can do this here now or back at the office, it's your choice."

"Alright, but get in my car, this doesn't look right. I have a lot of nosey neighbors, who take the Railroad."

"OK, Beatty."

One inside the car, Thomas can see that she is more nervous than he has ever seen her. He's not sure if he just caught her off-guard or is she guilty of something, he doesn't know about yet?

He is not looking forward to telling her the news.

"Beatty I have something to tell you." She looks at him as if he's going to say, that she is under arrest. Thomas continues *"James Arrondi ... is dead."* She foolishly tries to hide her emotions and says to him "I'm not familiar with a ..."

"Beatty, or should I say LORRAINE! Do you really want to tell me that you don't know him?"

"Lorra ... How did you find that out.?"

"You did a great job of covering your tracks, but it was James that told me."

"That means you spoke to him ... *When? ... Where?*"

"I spoke to him a couple of days ago at the safe house they were keeping him in. He was doing fine, just a little beat up."

"How was he ... I mean ...who ...*Who killed him?*"

"He was hit by a car, as he ran straight onto the main road, to avoid his captors."

"Was it over quickly? ... Did he suffer?"

"As far as I know, he didn't." She then breaks down and cries. It was as if she was crying for *all* the things in her life that had gone wrong. After a couple of minutes she stopped.

"I have to call my husband and tell him I'm running late and that I'll have to catch a later train. I just hope no one saw you enter my car tonight."

"Beatty, I need to ask you some questions and I really need you to be truthful with me."

"OK, I'll answer anything you want, just promise me you won't involve my family."

"Beatty, at this stage of the game, I really can't make that promise ..." His voice trailed off. He couldn't help, but feel drawn to her and her problems. There was something about her that just kind of drew you in. Thomas figured that was the reason that she was always mixed up with the wrong type of men in her life. He hoped that her husband was different than any of them.

"So, I need you to tell me if you had any involvement with supplying the evidence or the phone message in regards to when James was at the station house."

Sheepishly she said, "*I had no choice, but to help.*"

"What do you mean, you had no choice?" ... Did Dorland put you up to this?" She just nodded her head in a positive way.

"Tell me what you know about James?"

"I'm sure he told you everything ... well ... almost everything. Do you think it's possible to be in love with more than one person Thomas?"

"I never used to, but I'm starting to think it is."

"You see, I was in love with Matt Dorland. But he treated me so bad and then he cheated on me, over and over again Then James came along and he was so different and I fell for him. He made me realize that I was still young and need to get out of the situation I was in. The whole situation with Matt, the situation with being a working girl, the whole thing. "

Beatty poured out her heart to him. She had never told anyone what she was telling him now.

"But the sexual attraction to Matt Dorland, *never went away ...*"

She continued "There was just something magical when we were in bed together. So I straightened out my life and James caught us together one time and it broke his heart. He then went straight to drugs, drinking and gambling. I still wanted a normal life and because Matt came from the family he did, I could never be his wife."

Thomas was not so sure that Dorland would have consented to it anyway.

"So, one day at the job, I meet a real cute vendor who was honest and legit. Six months later, we were married. But I still snuck away to be with Matt, whenever I could.
As you know, I still see him. I lie to my husband, I lie to myself. But it's what I need to survive in this life. And, when my kids were born, Matt distanced himself from me 'cause he had lost and he didn't like it."
"So was that evidence all Dorlands ...
—and is he THE LONE RIDER?"
" I don't know what evidence you're talking about. I never saw anything, all I did was make the phone call."
"Beatty, do you know the Dorkins ... Paul and Charles?"

"Look Thomas, there's a cute small bar in the next town. Lets continue this there, 'cause I'm starving.
"Yeah! that would be great."
"Yeah, I'm having a really great time with you Thomas."

Odd thing to hear, when you're doing an investigation, he thought.

Chapter 29
The Seduction

[Thomas and Beatty make small talk and discover that they have a lot in common. They enjoy the same music, the same shows, even the same Politics.

Thomas finds that he has become attracted to her. She is equally attracted to him. Their conversation becomes less formal and more flirtatious.]

Lili's bar

Beatty calls her husband and inquires about her sick child.

"How is he? ... he's doing better! ... that's great Hon, listen I'm really going to be stuck at work and I think I'd be better off if I just stayed in the City. Are you sure you don't mind? OK, give them all my love. Talk to you tomorrow ... Lov ya!"

Beatty and Thomas grab some quick food and a couple of drinks and pretty soon, it's like they've known each other *forever!* When the bill comes, Beatty grabs it and pays for it with her credit card. Then she turns to Thomas and says ...

"Thomas look, I really like you and I would like to spend the night with you now, if you wouldn't object. I know you heard me tell my husband I wouldn't be home. *So lets go tear up some sheets.*" She says "I mean you are off-duty now, aren't you?'

"Yeah, I'm off-duty and it does seem like a wonderful idea, BUT ..."

"It's alright, you probably have a wife and a family, like I do and you ..."

"Beatty, what I was going to say was that I have to go and make a phone call too. That I also, will be working late and that I'll be staying in the City. I would like nothing better than to *tear-up the sheets* with you. There's something about you that I just find utterly intoxicating. Is there a place that we can go to that is really close by."

"Yes, there is a place just up the road from here." she says. "Why do you think I choose this place? And, besides there's a 24-hour liquor store across the street. My treat ... As they are leaving she opens her trunk and takes out a small travel bag."

Thomas thinks to himself that he's a real *bastard*, after all the trust and forgiveness that his wife has given him, He rationalizes what he's about to do, by saying to himself ...
"Look Thomas, you're not getting any younger or better looking. You're about to have to retire and as I see it, the rest of your life is sort-of over!

Why shouldn't I take advantage of the way the two of us feel at this moment? And I feel ALIVE! right now and I want to have ... No, I need to find comfort in this womens arms tonight."

Then, he thinks about his faith.

He knows the difference between bad and good etc. He tells himself that he has done much good and he will be forgiven for doing some bad ...

Wrong answer ...!

Chapter 30
The Stunt

4 Corners hotel

"Wait in the car Thomas, let me make the arrangements."

"Beatty, you paid for dinner, drinks and the wine and now the Hotel—are you trying to make me feel bad?"

"No!...Thomas, *I just make a lot more money, than you do* ... just being practical."

Thomas' pride is hurt, *but he'll live.*

Beatty comes back after a couple of minutes ...

"Honey, just thought I'd let you know what room number where in. Room 69 and I think that's just how we're going to get started.

I'm so WET...!!!"

[*What they don't know is that the Hotel clerk picks up the phone and calls, of all people, Detective Slinger.*]

Once in the room Beatty says to Thomas ...

"Thomas give me a moment, I just want have to freshen-up a little bit. Why don't you get naked and get under the covers. "Once in the bathroom, she makes a call on her cell-phone and calls Matt Dorland. "Hi Matt, listen I won't be able to make it tonight, my kid's sick and running a high fever."

"Matt says really, I'm sorry about that. Say, where are you now?"

"I just was on my way down to the station, on my way to the Railroad. I got stuck in work late. Hope you don't mind?"

"Well look, just make sure you make it here Friday night. I bought you a little something."

"Oh, Matt, you want to see me Friday?"

"Sure I do *Lorraine*! Goodnight!"

All of a sudden, she felt a knot in the pit of her stomach. Matt never ever, called her Lorraine ... Now, she was really frightened. Just then Thomas calls out—*Hey, did you forget about me?*"

"No Thomas", she says, "I'm just starting to change into a little something, from that bag that I took out of the car. I think you're going to like ... *make that love!* Shall I describe it to you, or should I just pop out and show it to you? "Why don't you describe it to me, so I can try to picture it and then when you 'pop' out, it will just make me crazier!"

"Well, this outfit is really frilly and absolutely see-through. It has a push-up bra that really shows off, my still really firm, full D-Cup breasts and features a crotch-less panty. The black color of the outfit is complimented, by my very pale skin and a set of F*** me shoes, My piercings will make you crazy and my four tattoo's will keep you intrigued. My perfume will arouse you and my tongue and hands will make sure that you never forget me!" She can't wait to show him, how good she still looks."

"ARE READY!?"
"Are you kidding?"

When she steps out of the bathroom, he is amazed at what he sees. The way she carries herself and the way her make-up is done —why it almost makes him think he's with different women. An even more beautiful women then she in fact, really is.

Thomas offers her a glass of wine in the plastic cups she bought and she proceeds to pour the wine over the front of her body.
"Opps! silly me Thomas, now I guess you're going to have to pour me another glass after you lick it off of me ... And don't forget to drink yours."

As she steps into bed, he rises to devour her. Soon they are in an *embrace* that knows no bounds! As they get more familiar with each other, they move around and switch positions until she is sitting on top of him. Withering and propelling herself up and down as if, she is never going to stop. They start to make those intense sounds that only lovers, in the heat of passion, make.

[*Unbeknownst to them, someone is 'jimming' the lock to their room and is about to burst in!*]

All of a sudden, Slinger throws the door wide open and one of his hands is behind his back, holding something. As he moves towards them, he starts to bring his hand forward. Thomas' instinct starts to take over, as he believes he has a gun. Thomas tries to push Beatty to the side (she actually spins around, looking straight at the intruder) as Thomas tries to shield her with his body.

Her first thought is that Dorland is going to have them killed!

Thomas thinks to himself, **not like Joseph and Scanner!**

Beatty is mortified and she can't help thinking that this is about that phone call, she made earlier, in the bathroom.

Slinger moves his hand to the front and points at them and *shoots!*

He shoots them **with a camera, not a gun!**

He shoots them several more times, then turns and flees. Thomas makes sure that Beatty is alright, then flings a pair of pants on and runs out the door, chasing after him. Slinger had a car waiting and makes good his *escape.*

"Slinger, You Bastard!"

There is nothing for Thomas to do now, but to go back to the room and try to console Beatty. She is in the room slumped in a corner with a blanket covering her. She keeps repeating to herself, through her tears ...

"Not   again!   Not   again!   I   will   not   be blackmailed again ... Never again!"

Thomas tries to comfort her, but she is just about in a total semi-catatonic state and really is oblivious to what he is saying, then she screams out loud.

"Oh My God—My Husband!
—What will become of my family!?"

Thomas sees a little life in her eyes return, he whispers to her "It's not about you Beatty, *it's about me*. You see that wasn't a reporter, that was a shitty Detective named Kip Slinger. Thomas says, as he continues to stroke Beatty's hair. Thomas knows she'll be alright, he just has to be patient with her.

"Slinger did that as a little insurance for himself. He knows that if I were caught in a compromising situation, he could use that to manipulate me, in my investigation."

She whispers weakly "I don't understand. Am I going to be OK, More importantly, is my family going to be OK!?"

After a couple more minutes, the Beatty of old comes back.
"Thomas, how did he know where to find you ... us?'
"I can only guess that the clerk downstairs gave him a heads up."

"But Thomas. it doesn't make sense–You never got out of the car! You never signed in! It wasn't your credit card that was used!"

"I don't exactly know how, but I know that what I just said, is probably how it happened. I just have a hunch, that's all"

"Anyhow Thomas, *come back to bed!*"

"*What!* Beatty are you sure you don't want to just go home or something."
"Look Thomas, this is one of those absolutely rare times when **I'M ACTUALLY PAYING FOR THE ROOM** for the night and I intend to get all my monies worth (*she licks her lips*)." Thomas looks happily surprised ...

"Besides the damage is already done and I don't think this guy Slinger is going to come back tonight Thomas. *Do you?*"

Thomas shakes his head negatively.

Beatty says to Thomas, as she stares into his eyes ...
"Besides, I didn't get all dressed up like this for nothing...!"

Chapter 31
The Deal

TaskForce HQ

Thomas shows up for work looking a little worse for wear.
He can't believe the stunt that Slinger pulled. Thomas has lost all respect for the man. That wasn't even worthy of a dime store mall cop. How could he sink so low?

Then, he sits back for a moment and thinks of the night he just had. *It doesn't get any better than that!* If he were to die today, at least he could say that he once in his life, had a night like that. It didn't even matter how much mileage she had on her. She knew how to treat a man. He says out loud ...

"No wonder she was so damm popular. Ha!"

RING! RRING! RRRING! RRRRRING!

Thomas picks up the phone on the fourth ring and says
   "What took you so long? You piece of shit!"
   "Relax Thomas, I'm sure you figured out why I did that."
   "YOU'RE SUCH A COWARD!"
   "No, Thomas, but I am a survivor. Remember, I'd like to retire someday, just like you're going to do..."
   "So, what do you want? What is this great plan and more importantly, who put you up to it? Was it Dorland? Was it his idea? For you to sink so low ... is just unimagineable. HOW MUCH?"
   "Well Thomas, I don't want to put any more pressure on you, but you have a little more than two weeks to solve the case."
   "And you want to help, right Slinger?" Thomas says that with more than a hint of disgust!
"In a way I do ... In a way I do ... You just don't understand it Banner, so many people have a piece of me now. It's getting so hard to keep them all happy. Used to be that on occasion, I just had to *bust a few heads* or look the other way." He continues venting to Thomas ...
   "Now-a-days, I get to just be a lousy Detective, a plainclothes

cop, a messenger, a servant, a politician, a priest, a daily confessor —well, you get the picture. And *who's looking out for me?*"

"So you got corrupted and now you want sympathy from me, forget it!"

"I'm not asking you to condone what I've done, I just want you to cooperate. That's all, just a little cooperation, a little professional courtesy. I don't want your money ..."

"HA!" Says Thomas.

"Thomas, since your deadline is approaching rather rapidly, 'We' just wouldn't want you to stumble on to anything that might cause 'Us' trouble. So 'We' just need you to back-off of the investigation and just let it unfold in whatever manner it will."

Slinger says this with a real authoritarian voice. "If you do that, those pictures will just be erased, but if you don't, they will be on the Internet and in The Daily Flush and other papers before you can say ... '*The Lone Rider'!*"

"So, what's with this 'We' stuff? Who's pulling your strings Slinger? Why can't you just say it's Dorland and be done with it?"

"Because Thomas believe it or not, it isn't."

Thomas thinks to himself, Ah! another 'county' heard from? But who the heck is it?

"You realize that if you release these pictures, you will be ruining not just two lives, but many."

"I bet Dorland would be really crushed about that ... I really could care less ... Banner—lay LOW on this case or else ...! Oh! and another thing, don't try to warn your boss or the department, or anyone else for that matter. Don't force me to do this! Think about the lady, if nothing else. Remember I have a hair-trigger on this so, if you do anything that pisses off my benefactor ... —they WILL get published."

"You realize that when this is all over, you and I have a score to settle. I told you I would bring you down."

"I've got other 'fish to fry' Banner. Good Luck!"

Chapter 32
The Question?

TaskForce HQ

Even though he expected the phone call to come and he kind of figured what the content would be, he never figured that Slinger would be protecting someone other than Dorland, but who?

RING! RRING!

"Hello Thomas, I just called to tell you how much I enjoyed the other night ... I took today off and I got to thinking."

She paused for a moment and then asked ...

"Have you heard from 'Our Friend' from the other night?
Has he made any demands? Is there anything I can do for you ... to help you, etc?"

"No, I can handle this, but I may need your help later." There is one more thing to ask of you, he said.

"I understand that this may be a real tough one for you, given the timeframe and all. But could you give me, as best you can remember, a list of names of clients you had back in the day. I would like to run it across one of our databases and see if there's a match with anyone, we might have on file?"

"Thomas that was so long ago and to be honest, there were *so many!* ... I'm not sure I'd even know where to start?"

"What about that madam, maybe she left a book of clients from her establishment. You know Carole something."

"Yes Thomas, I KNOW WHO SHE IS ... I'll try."

"Well, if you find out anything please, get it to me, ASAP."

She hesitated and then she said ...

"I don't know if this will help or not, but there was this guy Charlie. He was a little weird, even by my standards. Some of the girls were really afraid of him. But he always paid extra to get what he wanted. Real kinky stuff—that's what he was into. So mostly he came to me, for a couple of years.

Anyhow, years later I'm there, in a little Art House, watching an independent movie and whose name should come up, but this Charlie fellow, as one of the producers of the movie. I mean, I'm not even sure if it's the same guy, but it sounded kind of familiar, because Dorland was really pissed at this guy at the time, I think Matt even owed him money, if I recall."

"Beatty, this is really important ....! Do you remember the last name of this fellow?"

"Doors ... something? I think it was Dorrrs ... sounds like shins or something, Doorshins?"

"Beatty could it be Dorkins?"

"DORK-ins?"

"No Beatty DOR-kins, not DORK-ins!."

"I'm not really sure, but that sounds kinda right."

"Do you remember the name of the film?"

"Wow! It was quite awhile ago and I've seen so many movies since."

"Oh! Wait a minute, now I remember, I think it was called "Station Break/Broken?"

Then, there is a long pause and she says, "it was a love story about a couple and a set of trains and some erotic toys and it was filmed in our system. Of course, we would NEVER have allowed such a thing, if we had any idea it was happening. Still ...
—I can't believe what they got away with, in that film."

"Thanks Beatty, that's a start. It was great to hear from you. I was wonder ..."

"No, Thomas, as great as that was, I don't think now is a good time. You know I'm still frightened, and the deadline is about two weeks away and you still don't have anyone in your crosshairs. Do you Thomas?"

"Well, to tell you the honest truth, No!

But I'm sure with the information you just gave me, I should be able to come up with something. Don't worry, there's still time ...!"

Chapter 33
The Friend

Waterfront

Thomas pulls his car up to an empty space by the dock. Sometimes Thomas comes here to clear out his head. He came here a lot when Joseph was killed. It helped to clear his mind and ease him back from the brink of 'madness'.

First:

He needed to sort out what the story with Beatty is. That ones too easy, he thought to himself. It's just complicated, maybe too complicated? Should I tell Christine what has happened?, Should I just leave? And, what about how this will affect my sons? And most important, what about Beatty???

DOES SHE FEEL THE SAME WAY ...?

Second:

In just about two weeks time, I need to catch, what has so far has been uncatchable—a *suspect!*

Third:

How do I deal with all the pressure from my boss Peters, the Governor, the Mayor, the Public, The Daily Flush and the Internet and everything else?

Fourth:

What to do about Slinger and the blackmail threat? How do I proceed, without triggering, the release of those pictures?

And, how do I bring Slinger down? Although he's so corrupt, he'll probably do it to himself.

Thomas just sat by the ocean and gazed out. For a moment or two, all his trouble just seemed like they were yesterdays news. Like he had not a care in the world. He truly was in a blissful state.

BUZZ! BBUZZ! BBBUZZ!

Just then, he gets snapped back to reality, when he receives a phone call from Beatty. How about that for timing?

"Hello lady, How are You?"

"Thomas listen, I need you to meet me at the Horse-White Tavern in about twenty minutes. There's someone I'd like you to meet."

"Sure Beatty, I'll be there."

Horse-White Tavern

Thomas arrives and is greeted by Beatty and another woman.

"Thomas, I'd like you to meet a real good friend of mine named Gwen Blissing, I've told her all about you" Thomas wasn't sure if that was personally or professionally, or both.

"Hello, Gwen"

"Thomas, Gwen is a friend of mine, in fact, we go way back. Back to the days of Carole Sheets. The funny thing is she worked there too—but as the *bookkeeper*."

Thomas checks her out. She is a well preserved woman with short pixieish dark hair, with a very slim body. She seems kind of mousey and demure. OK looking, but nothing great.

"Anyhow Thomas, I did as you requested and made a list of names (she hands Thomas a folded piece of paper). There's really not a lot of names on it, but Gwen has got a great memory and she knew a lot about what went on there, back in the day."

"Lorraine! Opps, I mean Beatty, I can't belive that's the name you go by nowadays! It's just hard to get used to."

"Thomas says. "As you know Gwen, I'm looking for names, I want you and Beatty to take a look at this list and see if there's anyone's name that you might recognize ...?"

```
        Jesse Knight
   Carlos & Winston Allcus
        Kip Slinger
   Charlie & Paul Dorkins
      Betty Morgenstern
        Matt Dorland
        Doc Redin
```

"Who'd you get this list from Thomas and why is my name on it?" Beatty knows why, because she was at that meeting with Slinger and Dorland and those others.

"I'm not sure why you're on it, but one of my sources gave it to me."

"Yeah whatever, anyhow I know Jesse Knight. He was one of my clients, back in the day.

"Mine too," says Gwen

"Wait a minute, I thought you were the bookkeeper!?"

"Well back then, I was discovering my sexual self. I even turned a few tricks on the side, just for the thrill of it. And he definitely was one of them, but he wasn't in the service—he was just a special customer." She seems to be relishing the memories, as she spoke to Thomas. "And, Beatty was the *first* woman I ever went to bed with. We even did a threesome together once, which was quite FANTASTIC!"

When she said that, and she had the biggest grin on her face. like the *'cat who ate the canary'*...

"I think you're exaggerating a touch there Gwen. After all, I was there too." Beatty says. "Although we did get payed a great deal of money for that one, didn't we?"

Thomas could not believe what he was hearing. Nobody would have suspected her of such behavior, that's for sure. I mean with her short hair and those big glasses, she looked more like a school teacher, than a 'part-time' hooker.

"And there was another fellow, I'm pretty sure. Beatty do you remember him or did this happen after you left...?

Well, there was this kid that was in the service, as a medic and he said that he always wanted to be a doctor, ever since he was a kid in school. His last name was Redin ... Hank Redin, but everybody just called him 'Red'."

"I'm pretty sure he did become a doctor. Yeah, that's right. He had a big party with Rita and Anne." She looked at Beatty and Thomas as if to say that's all I know."

"Gwen, you didn't mention Slinger or Dorland, how come?"

"Oh! I just figured that Beatty had mentioned those two when she talked to you, that's all. Well listen guys, I really have to run and get back to my job. If you need anything else, just call me" After she leaves Thomas asks ...

"So what *'job'* is that!?"

"She still a bookeeper, if that's what you mean, Thomas?

"Anyhow Beatty, it really is *great* to see you!"

"Yes, it's great to see you too ..."

"Beatty, you were at that meeting with all those others and I was wondering why you were there and what exactly was the meeting about?" you could just feel the tension enter the room, like a 'wet blanket'."

"That's great Thomas, we haven't seen each other in while and the first thing you do, when we're alone, is go right back into the job. I didn't realize how cold you could be ..."

"Beatty be reasonable. You know I'm running out of time and I need all the answers I can get."

"Well, I'm not going to stand for it, I'm getting out of here." She attempts to leave and Thomas grabs her wrist and gently prevents her from leaving. He looks at her as if to say please don't leave. She sits back down.

"Beatty I need an answer to my question. Why were you there?"

"I was there because Matt asked me to go."

"Alright, but what was the meeting about."

"I *can't* tell you that Thomas ..."

"Beatty—*I need to know this.*"

"Thomas I understand, but what you don't understand, is that these are not the type of people that you want to get on the wrong side of."

"BEATTY I"M NOT GOING TO ASK YOU AGAIN!"

"*Thomas, please keep your voice down.*" She pleaded for Thomas to remain calm.

"Well you see Thomas, EVERYONE at that meeting, including me were involved one way or the other, with the Transit thing, and the ClickCard thing and the concrete thing and other stuff and..." she was shaking now. And, tears just started to stream down her eyes. There was no sounds, no demonstrative motions—they just came pouring out of her eyes!

"Beatty do you know if anyone at that meeting is The Lone Rider? That's really all I need to know now. As to the rest of what you told me, I think I could have figured most of those things out myself."

"Thomas, I'm not really sure. For the longest time and with the way he's been acting, I thought it must be Dorland."

"What changed your mind."

"The murders of Rimsum and those others."

Chapter 34
The Split

Horse-White

"So you're saying that those murders convinced you that Dorland wasn't involved—how so?"

"What convinced me was that trip I made with Dorland out to Las Vegas."

"When was that Beatty"

"It was awhile ago. Anyhow, on occasion I have to go to seminars on new products and when I told Matt that I was going, he said he'd like to go too. That way we could make a little vacation out of it. Sometimes, he would just surprise me with things like that. Trips, gifts—you know, things a woman just loves." then she said wistfully, "great idea until I really thought about it."

"What do you mean Beatty."

"Well, Las Vegas isn't exactly the kind of place you bring a person with a *gambling* problem, now is it?"

"I guess not" Thomas said

"Well anyhow, he promised me that the trip would just be about us and that he would hardly do *any* gambling ... and I believed him." She sounded so sad.

"Well, it was to be a real long weekend trip, four days of FUN and we even went first-class, when they found out he was coming back, they laid out the red-carpet for us *again!*"

"You had been there before?"

"Sure, lots of times. we stayed at the *best* Hotels, drank the *best* wine, saw the *best* shows and had the largest suite they could provide. Whatever he wanted, trust me, he got! Sometimes they even provided some other women and men to play with—*if you get my drift?*" She says all of this, as if she was remembering it with very fond memories. As if to say, look, this is who I am and I'm not ashamed to say it.

Anyhow, Beatty says. "that on the first two nights that she was there, everything was terrific. He got to gamble, while I was at the seminars and he managed to control himself—win, lose or draw. Whatever time we said that we would meet up, we did. We went to dinner, he bought me new clothes, all designer stuff and he bought me the most incredible diamond and sapphire bracelet with matching earings. I was truly living the dream until ..."

"Until what Beatty?" Thomas really didn't want to hear all of this. It felt somewhat similar to when he was doing those interviews with those people from Transit. There was just something about the way she spoke that just fascinated him. Then she said to him ...

"So, are you still listening Thomas."

"Sure I am Beatty."

"Well, he had the worst thing happen to him that you can have happen to a gambler. He got lucky! *He got really LUCKY!* Now, I don't know if the Casino was just setting him up, or what, but he just couldn't leave the table. For the most part he gambled for almost 32 hours straight! No food, a couple of drinks and that was it. And I was going out of mind, with worry and BOREDOM!

Sure in the beginning it was fun, it was exciting, it was thrilling, and then it just got *boring*! When you win on almost every bet for hours and hours at a time—it's just the most boring thing in the World ..."

"Then, he hit a stretch where he started to lose a little and he must have been starving by then.Well, we actually left the table and we had the most incredible romantic dinner for two you could imagine in our room."

"Then what happened Beatty?"

"Well, after that meal and the champagne, all I can tell you is *nothing makes a gambler more horny than winning*, so for the next two hours we did everything you could imagine, but hang upside down from the ceiling. I was totally exhausted—but not him."

So, I'm thinking he's going to mellow out, keep the winnings and we'd get to go home winners. And that's what looked like was going to happen, then he gets a phone call. She said she couldn't hear all of the conversation, but that a friend of his was in town and that he was sitting at a table that was running *hot* and that was all he needed to hear ... then something strange happened after the phone call was over.

"He said to me Beatty, I need you to do me a little favor. I'm going to go downstairs and give you more then half the money I've won so far and I want you to send fifty thousand dollars to Charlie Dorkins and then I want you to go Downtown as soon as you can and open up several bank accounts in the name of James Arrondi.

And I want you to send some money to these accounts that he already has. AND I want you to call my friend Brenda Craig to arrange it (He hands her a piece of paper with all the information she needs)."

 She couldn't believe what she was hearing—"he was putting money into savings accounts for JAMES!?
 Is this really suppose to be some kind of a crazy joke Matt? BECAUSE I DON'T THINK ITS *very funny!*"

He looked at her in such a way that she knew that he was very serious.
 "Why? Why would you do it? You hate James and you've never forgiven me for leaving you when I did. You know, I wouldn't do anything to hurt James, ever!"
 "Beatty, YOU *WILL* DO THIS and you will not question why, —**JUST OBEY!**

Because, you know what will happen if you don't." Matt is already dressed and as he's about to leave he turns to her and says, *"are you coming or not, Beatty?"*

 "He had too much on me and I couldn't take the chance that he would ruin things for my family and me, so I went. On the ride in the elevator, he explained to me how he planned to set James up and that I would have to do everything he demanded or *I would suffer the consequences!*"

And, then she got really angry, as if this was a movie and she knew how the ending turns out, before the rest of the audience does.

She hated herself for what she would be doing to James and she hated Matt and at that moment, she just hated her life.

—more than she ever did, when she was turning tricks!

Chapter 35
The Truth

Horse-White

"So what happened next Beatty, please continue."

"When we went down to the Hotel and he cashed in about 65 percent of his winnings and got the hotel to write a couple of checks, just as he instructed them to do. Then, he went back to the Casino to meet his friend and I went about the errands that he wanted me to do. Well, it took a little longer than I thought and by the time I got back, he had lost most of his money, playing craps.

"So you guys took off and you discovered what?

"No, As soon as I got back, he asked if I had deposited all the checks? I said that I had followed his instructions to the letter."He seemed quite irritable and angry and then he asked me to go back to our room and get something for him.

"What did he want Beatty?"

"He wanted me to go and get that beautiful bracelet and matching earrings that he had given me. And do you know what that S.O.B wanted me to do? He told me that I was to go to a pawn shop on the strip and try and get as much money as possible for them—*because he was starting to feel lucky again!*"

Matt had lost all reason by then and no matter how she pleaded with him to stop—it was to no avail. He was truly in the grip of his addiction.

"That's the worst thing you can ever hear from a gambler!"

"Well, I went upstairs to my room and I packed my bag, crying. I then called room service and had them bring up a scissor."

"Why would you want one? I don't understand?"

"They brought one to me and ...

I proceed to cut-up every stitch of his clothing that Matt had in the room, EVERYTHING—socks, underwear, suits ties etc.
I took all of the cut up clothing and packed it inside his luggage.

I then went and got as much money as I could for the jewelry, just like he had instructed. I gave it to him (minus money to get home) and then said I was going back up to the room, to lie down for awhile." She continued.

"I then arranged for them to bring down my bags and I proceeded to hail a cab and go to the airport, to take the next available flight home. I just didn't give a damn anymore ..."

[*As it turned out, the person Dorland went to meet at the Casino was Max Dorman. It seems that Max liked to gamble too. He was the one that talked Dorland into playing craps.*

Dorland was feeling Lucky and considering he was down about half a million dollars, he really needed to win. He did start to and eventually got to the point when he was losing less then thirty grand—which he considered **winning.** *He left the Casino carrying a promissory note from the hotel and caught a plane ride with Max.*

Oh, and when Dorland saw his clothes were missing from the closet, at first he thought they had been robbed! When he saw her luggage was gone, he opened up his suitcases ... **all he did was laugh!** *He had a tailor come to the room and had new clothes by the evening flight.*]

"So, you stop seeing him after that?

"You know I couldn't do that. I'm as addicted to him, as he is to gambling. I'm so addicted to him that after you and I had that great time in bed ..." *She chose her next words carefully ...*

"Well, I took the next day off, so I could get back in bed with him! I'm really very sorry Thomas, but that's who I am—it's not a very pretty picture—is it!"
Thomas was stunned, hurt, confused and angry. But he didn't say anything, he didn't have to.

She could see it in Thomas' eyes. She had seen that look before, in other men's eyes ... that she had hurt really badly.

"Beatty ... I ... don't know what to say ... I was planning to ..."

"I know Thomas and I would have loved to hear what you had to say, but you see I'm just that type of woman, *bad to the bone.*"

Thomas was so far gone at that moment, that he easily could have *killed* her OR *loved* her even more.

Chapter 36
The Revelation

TaskForce HQ

The last thing that Beatty told Thomas was that she was really sorry and that she really could have fallen for him with her heart and given him the use of her body, but ... she would *always* be Matt's woman.

Thomas was glad that he had left the bar when he did.

In a way, her revelation was a great relief to him! He would always have that great memory of their night together and he would be able to salvage his marriage—*maybe!?*

Now he must get back on track with the investigation. He had Gwen's number and wanted to give her a call about those people that she knew on his list.

"Hi Gwen, this is Special Agent Thomas ..."

"I certainly remember you Thomas. What's on your mind?"

"I just wanted to know a little more about Dorkins and Redin. so, whatever you can remember, might be of great help—even the smallest detail might mean something."

"Ok, this Redin fella was into pretty much vanilla stuff. What he lacked in size, he made up in stamina.

"Did he ever get into any kind of real trouble while he was at Carole's?" Thomas inquired and waited for her response.

"Only one time. I remember there was some trouble when he celebrated his graduation from Med school. He had this big party with a couple of friends and I guess they got a little carried away and the next thing you know a brawl breaks out over Rita and he gets caught in the middle of it, because of some misunderstanding.

Well, he wound up with a broken nose and lots of bruises and was really about to get creamed, by one of the bouncers there, when Slinger interceded on his behalf—*probably saved his life.* I'm betting he never forgot that." She thought about it some more, while Thomas had to sit there and wait patiently on the phone, until she said ...

"Well that's about it on him ... as to the other guy"

"Yeah! What do you know about Charlie Dorkin."

""That guy was a whole different trip. I mean this guy was into EVERYTHING! The kinkier the better and he had lots of money to throw around. He might hire two or three girls a night. He was into whips and chains and anything you could think of." Thomas imagined from her tone of voice, that she had a look of disgust on her face.

"And man this guy had a piece of equipment larger than you'd ever see in any porn movies. And he used to hire really small girls AND GUYS. You know, they say size matters, but this dude, he really LIKED to cause or receive extreme pain and with that room divider in his pants, he often did! One time I even gave him a try and I couldn't walk without pain, for about two weeks, but I LOVED IT!"

"OK! Gwen, that just about does it. Did you think of anyone else that you might have come across?"

"YEAH, come to think of it there was this really tallish guy named Lou Long. I hear he went to work for Transit after a number of years on his own. I also heard that he had a about four kids, with different women, that he raised them like little disciples. Anyhow, He had a bunch of citations and medals and he would spend time with some of the girls here, but mostly he'd just get drunk and talk about his experiences in the war. So for every time he got laid, there were two or three times that he just paid the women to listen. Kind of pathetic, don't you think? Anyhow he was a very sharp guy who on occasion would come in, and *pretend,* that he was out of his mind—just for the FUN of it!"

"Ok Gwen, that's some great stuff. Think I'll see if I can use the information you provided to further the investigation. Thanks again." "Feel free to call me anytime Thomas, Goodbye."

Chapter 37
The Deadline

Dorlands' apartment

Thomas decided that he was going to stake-out Dorlands apartment and as soon as Dorland got home, he was going to pay him a visit.

He thought about it in the car and realized that no matter what direction the investigation took, it always came back to Dorland. He either instigated, or enabled or covered up everything.

This particular visit was going to get ugly and he was prepared for that. And, for the consequences that would ensue, in the aftermath of that visit. Meanwhile, in todays headline in the paper, he just couldn't get it out of his mind ...

THE DAILY FLUSH

DEADLINE LOOMS OVER US ALL!!!

ONE HUNDRED THOUSAND DOLLAR REWARD!!!
for information related to the apprehension anytime of a suspect in the THE LONE RIDER case—**before** September 17, 2011!

The Daily Flush has generously *DOUBLED* the current reward in hopes that this might spur someone on, to help us in the prevention of this crime.

Afterfall, there was only a week before the deadline now and
if he was going to get any more answers, he was going to have to 'shake the tree' a bit.
Thomas has been in the car a little over an hour, when Dorland steps out of a cab with a young blonde woman. They passionately kiss and then she gets back in the cab and it takes off into the night. Dorland proceeds to stop and talk to the doorman and then goes into the building.

Thomas gets out of his car and starts to cross the street. All of a sudden, he feels a vibration in his pants pocket ...

BUZZ! BBUZZ! BBBUZZ!

"Hello Thomas ... hope I'm not disturbing you?
"Well to tell you the truth Christine, I was right in the middle of something ..."
"I'm sorry, but I need you to do something for the boys."
"Right now, you mean it can't wait?" Thomas said.

BEEP BBEEP BBBEEP BBBEEP BEEP BBEEP

"Hold on Hon, I'm getting another call. I'll call you right back, I promise." Thomas takes the other call, he doesn't recognize the number ...
"Hello, who's this?"
"Is this Special Agent Thomas Banner?"
"Yes it is ... and to whom am I speaking to?"
"My name is Mr. Chim, and I would like to speak with you about a most *urgent* matter."
"What is this in reference to, Mr. Chim?"
"I'd rather not say over the phone, but if you could find your way clear to meet with me now, I'm sure it will be worth your time and effort."
"So, how did you get my cell number?"
"I am a man of means Mr. Banner and if I want something there usually is someone willing to provide such, for a price. If not, then some form of persuasion usually works,"
"Which one did you use this time Chim?"
"Oh, the latter Mr. Banner, definitely the latter."
"Where would you like to meet Mr. Chim."
"I have a suite Downtown at the Hotel across from the Railroad. If you just let me know your location, my driver will come and pick you up and bring you here."
"How do I know this isn't some kind of a set-up."
"It's very simple Mr. Banner, if you don't come then I can not be responsible for what happens, to Ms. Blissing ...!"

Thomas feels a chill go down his spine. That poor woman, he can't let anything happen to her. Thomas gives Mr. Chim his location and says let me talk to her OR I'm not going ...

"Mr Banner that would indeed be foolish and unnecessary, I assure you, she is alive, but if you decide not to come ... well then, that's a whole different story then, isn't it. Well, Special Agent Banner, what are you going to do?"

Thomas gives Chim's driver his location over the phone and he is told he will be picked-up in fifteen minutes. Thomas then calls his wife, who he knows is going to just be furious ...

"Hi Christine ... I know your not picking the phone up because you're pissed. You're going to be even more pissed because I just can't do what you need me to—I'm really SORRY! This is matter of life and death that I'm dealing with and I just don't have the time. If you listen to this message, please, please call me back, so I can explain ..."

"Oh SHIT!" Thomas says out loud, "my damm cell-phone needs to be recharged again or something!" Frustrating piece of junk, doesn't matter that it's over ten years old. Sometimes it works, others times it doesn't. Thomas thinks to himself.

At that moment a black stretch limousine pulls up to the curb where he is standing. He gets in and in practically no time, he is at Mr. Chim's Hotel. He gets out and proceeds to the elevator and goes in and presses the Penthouse button, as instructed.

Chim's suite
Thomas thinks to himself that this is a darn fine Hotel that he has never been inside before. They have done a wonderful job with the decor. And then he is trying to figure how this 'Mr. Chim' figures into the puzzle of this investigation.

He gets out and proceeds to the ornate door down the hall, knocks, and enters into this enormous two bedroom suite.

"Nice of you to join us this evening. Mr. Banner."
"Skip the small talk Mr. Chim. I want to see Ms. Blissing and I DEMAND to see her now!"

"I think first, we need to talk Special Agent Thomas Banner again I give you my word, that she is fine."
"Then bring her out to me."
Mr. Chin nods to an associate, who proceeds to go into one of the

bedrooms. Thomas hopes he went to get Gwen.

[*Mr. Chan Chim, a very distinguished, very, very wealthy, very handsome fifty something year old businessman. With holdings all over the world, He is looking to expand his empire and to his collection of one-offs. Rare, one of kind things, like exotic cars... birds ... jewelry ... and businesses. Anything, that only he could possess, was of interest to him.*

It is said that he will spare no expenses or effort to get what he desires. He owns or operates businesses from Casino's to some leading Nanotech companies. He has managed to keep a very low profile, unless he believes it is necessary to intercede into a situation to come to a resolution, in his favor.

He is an engineer by trade and a Buff by nature. Many people are beholding to him and those who have tried to cross him, are usually never heard from again.]

Thomas looks around the room and sees three very beautiful women dressed in evening gowns and four men who appear to be bodyguards. Two of the men appear to have suffered injuries, as if they had been in a fight and lost.

Mr. Chim says to Thomas "I understand that you have come into possession of something that I want. I could send my men for it, but it would take to much time, so I thought, if I asked you for it nicely—*you might provide it to me."*

Thomas looks amused ..."*I have something you want?* You're kidding right? Judging by the looks of things, there isn't much that you don't already have. So what is it?"

Mr. Chim motions to another one of his henchman, who appears to be moving closer to Thomas. The first associate then reappears with Gwen Blissing. She is bound and gagged and looks like she has been through hell!

"What have you done to her? If you hurt her ..."

"It's not what we have done to her, it is what she did to two of my best men. The ones that were supposed to protect me?"

One of the guards pulls down the handkerchief that was around Gwen's mouth and she says rather loudly and with an attitude.

"YEAH, I KICKED THEIR ASSES!!!"

"Do not give yourself too much credit Ms. Blissing, because after all we did get you to give up Banners' number." Mr. Chim says with an air of superiority.

Gwen says "Oh Yeah, I don't think it would have turned out that way, if it was a fair fight—*do you?*"

One of the men motions to hit her. Mr. Chim turns to him and says to him in a very serious manner. "STOP, If you dare strike her

—you will forfeit your life."

"Anyhow, judging by the type of man I think you are, I brought her out, so that we could take care of the business at hand.

Special Agent Thomas Banner, think very carefully about the answer to the question I am about to ask you. Remember, your life, Ms. Blissings' life and the life of your family hangs in the balance." Mr. Chim's enforcers are showing Thomas that they are packing heat. His women have gathered around Mr. Chim, caressing and fondling him, as he speaks ...

"It is my understanding that you carry around with you a list. A very, very particular list. A list with the names of people who participated in some clandestine meetings. **I WANT THAT LIST!**

"OH! that list. I left it at the office ... " he says ...

"I know you are lying. You can give it to me yourself OR I can have my men search you for it. Unfortunately, I can't promise that you will still be in one piece, if I do that.

Quite simply the choice is yours Banner"

Thomas puts up a brave front and says, "Oh Yeah, just let them try ..."

"Banner who are you kidding? Perhaps you would prefer if we just take it out on Ms. Blissing?"

"I don't think *she* OR *your men* are going to like that either! Besides enlighten me, what do you need that list for?"

Chapter 38
The Escape?

Chim's

Thomas keeps talking, working the angles, trying to figure out how he might find the right moment, to make his move and get the drop on these guys.

"Well Banner, if you must know ..."

Thomas knows it's not a good sign when the bad guy starts telling you his plan. It usually means that he's planning on killing you now or *real soon.*

"... As I was saying, if you must know. At some point in time, one of my many companies bought a series of businesses in your country. One of them happened to be a company called Anvil2 Concrete."

He continues, as if he's really bored and as if he should not have to explain his actions to anyone.

"The company was actually bought, just so we could review their records on a rare element called Zinium ... *and where to find it exactly!"*

*"You bought an entire company just to review their records. And, I had hoped you might be a **smarter** businessman than that!"*

Mr. Chim looks at him indignantly, "I also became aware of their use of this element Zinium, in a one-of-a-kind 'ClickCard'. Therefore, it automatically became of interest to me. I then took a series of steps via my associates, to set about acquiring this Collectible. It seems that I have been very close many times, but someone or something has thus far prevented me from laying my hands upon it. Many lives have been taken in search of this quest and I will not hesitate to add to that number now, if I have to. Of course, you can help prevent all of this if you just cooperate."

Just then Thomas' phone starts to unexpectantly ...

RING! RRING! RRRING!
Excuse me , but I really need to get this call—it's probably my
wife ...

With that Thomas reaches into his pocket and pulls out his other weapon, a 45 caliber pistol. Apparently, much to his surprize, he has gotten the drop on them.

Mr. Chim says "Thomas, Ms. Blissing already has given up two of the people on the list. A Mr. Dorland and a Detective Slinger." Good girl Gwen, Thomas thinks to himself, she didn't really give him much and yet she managed to tell the truth.

"OK Mr. Chim, this is how this is going to play out. You are all going to back away. You're going to release Ms. Blissing and untie her. Then you're going to tell your men NOT to do anything stupid ... ARE WE CLEAR ON THAT? Do it now!"

Mr. Chim instructs his men on what to do and Gwen is untied.

"One last thing Chim, I am going to tell my guys and the local police what happened here and you guys will be brought up on charges for kidnapping and a host of other activities."

"Nothing has happened here, right Ms. Blissing? Not after I give you my word that ONE HUNDRED THOUSAND DOLLARS will be deposited in your account by tomorrow."
Thomas says to Mr. Chim, "that's not going to work ..."

Gwen says "You're right Thomas, make it THREE HUNDRED THOUSAND, *for each of us!*"

Mr. Chim is not happy, but after a long pause says ...
"**DONE!** You have my word."

Thomas is beyond words. This Gwen, is alright in his book.

Chapter 39
The Money

Chim's

Gwen turns to Thomas and says "Let's get the hell out of here. NOW! Thomas. Come on ... move man!"

Later as they hail a cab back to Thomas'car, Gwen puts her spin on what just happened.

"Look Thomas, I'm really no worse for wear and neither are you. We're alive and he won't go back on his word. It's that 'Code of Honor' thing. Lord knows my bank account could use a *'couple more zero's'* What about yours?"

"Gwen, you know we can't just take that money! He did threaten my family too. remember?"

"HE'S NOT GOING TO DO ANYTHING, UNDERSTAND!"

She said "I mean, you've got a family and bills and such. And, I can't imagine that the money couldn't help with that retirement of yours ...

Thomas thinks to himself, this is just one of those moments in life just like that moment of weakness, when you went with Beatty. —Take the money and you're on 'Easy Street' 'til you die."

The cab drops them off, right by Thomas car. "Gwen get in the car and I'll drop you home." She says "No, don't bother, I'm going to meet up with some friends. I'm going to take tomorrow off, so I can check my bank account."

Gwen gives Thomas a hug and says "Thanks for saving my life back there," Thomas laughs and says "Thanks for adding to my bank account. I guess, we'll talk tomorrow."

It then dawns on Thomas that his wife, never called him back. Or, maybe she did, but my cell-phones 'dead as a door nail' now.

I guess she's probably still mad at me and It's too late to go home, so—I guess I'll just go to the office and sleep. It'll be morning in a couple of hours and I'm exhausted!

TaskForce HQ

Thomas goes into his office, takes off his coat and lays down on the couch and says to himself "I guess I'll stake out Dorland again tonight ..." His last thoughts before falling asleep are ...

WOW! Three Hundred Grand! Seems like a ... dream!

Chapter 40
The Politics

TaskForce HQ

RING RRING! RRRING!

About two hours into his sleep, Thomas gets a phone call from his wife. She says "I didn't think you'd ... be here. I was going to leave you a voicemail that *I want a divorce!*

I'm not going put up with all this worrying and all this crazinesss. I'm taking the boys and I'm leaving you Thomas. I'll let you know where I am in a couple of days, so that you can see the boys, I'm sorry, really ... I tried, but I just can't take it anymore. Goodbye!"

Thomas, half-asleep, can not believe what he has heard. He has turned ghost-white and feels numb.

RING RRING! RRRING!

"Banner, this is Dorland."
"This is a little early even for you, isn't it?"
"I understand that you visited a business acquaintance of mine, last night. I just want to advise you that it would be in your best interest to provide to him, what he has requested from you."
"Well, that's right nice of you to do that Dorland" he says sarcastically.
"OK Banner, don't say you weren't warned!"
Dorland hangs up the phone and Thomas attempts to go back to sleep. Imagine the nerve of that guy. Like a call from him would have changed my mind.

RING RRING! RRRING!

"Thomas this is Gwen, I just want you to know that I'm walking out of my bank with **THREE HUNDRED GRAND!** credited to my account ..." I'm walking outside now, and I'm going to just SCREAM out loud!" Thomas is so *happy* for her ...
"Oh My God!" She says in a scream of absolute joy! "I CAN'T BELIEVE IT, he actually ..."

SISHPOP!

The phone sounds like it has hit the ground ...

... and them he hears people screaming and somebody says "Quick, call an ambulance! Somebody, HELP please!"

"Gwen, GWEN can you hear me? OH! NO, Gwen!!!"

Thomas' heart is in his mouth. He's pretty sure that the sound he heard was from a silencer. The worst has happened. Mr. Chim has kept his word alright. *And exacted his revenge!*

Once again, Thomas takes out his list ...

Deceased

Joseph Sorelo
Scanner Simmons
Ronald Rimsum
(& 2 men and a woman)
Carlos Allcus
Christopher Drake
James Arrondi
Gwen Blissing

TaskForce HQ
(thirty minutes later)

RING!
"It's Beatty Thomas ... Have you heard what just happened? GWEN IS DEAD! I can't believe she's dead! A friend of mine called me and told me the news. She told me that she was shot once —*in the head!* How could this happen and *do you know anything else about it?"*
"There's an investigation going on, I won't know how or why it happened as of this moment ... Beatty, don't cry ..."
Thomas tries to comfort her by telling her that he will "make some inquires."
"Thomas you must find out what happened, promise me. I just

know it had something to do with her helping us."

"I will try Beatty, now let me see if I can try and find out exactly what has happened."

"Thank you Thomas, I feel better already. Just knowing that you are going to look after her."

RING RRING! RRRING! RRRRING!

Thomas thinks to himself, it's going to be one of those days where I can't even get up to get a cup of coffee.

"Special Agent Banner ... my name is Jessie Knight and I need your HELP! You got to protect me ... and if you do, I'll tell you everything I know about THE LONE RIDER!"

"Where are you? Why don't you come to the TaskForce building and come up and see me?"

"You don't understand, I got these two guys after me and they're going to KILL ME!"

Thomas could hear the panic in his voice—he knew this guy was in trouble ...

"Can you meet me at the Museum of the Transit? Be there in about thirty minutes, Banner."

"Why meet there?"

"Because it will be right under their noses, so they won't think of going there."

"Alright, I'm on my way ..."

Thomas grabs his coat and heads out the door. Thomas knows that Jessie is the owner of the Anvil2 Concrete Company. He also knows that he was at those meeting, late at night, at the company.

Thomas hasn't been to that Museum since his kids were little. He remembers that they really loved it there, or rather the toys they got from the souvenir shop.

Museum of the Transit

Thomas gets there a couple of minutes late, traffic is just crazy at this time of day. He goes in and waiting for him is Jesse Knight (a tall, dark haired distinguished man with glasses, dressed real sharp and probably in his early sixties. Looks strong too.)

"You in the habit of being late, when someone needs your help? I mean I've been waiting for almost ten minutes. "

"Too Bad! I'm here man, lets just get on with it."

"Right to the point. I LIKE THAT!

"I don't care what you like! Tell me what you know about THE LONE RIDER."

"First, I want to be placed under your custody, to protect me from these guys and their associates."

Who the heck are you afraid of?"

"There are two guys looking to get rid of me. A Mr. Chim ... and his friends and a Detective named ..."

"Let me guess, Slinger."

How did you know that."

"It figures!"

"Anyhow, I just barely got away from Mr. Chim's guys a little earlier this morning and Slinger's working with Mr. Chim. He *used* to work for me. That dirty rat!"

"Guess he didn't like the split you were offering him ..."

"How did you know about that too?

"Doesn't matter. You're a big, strong guy and you got money to hire your own protection.Why do you need me?

"If there's one thing I've learned, it's that *you guys can't be bought* and anybody I hire, can be."

(Thomas thinks to himself, if he only knew, that I was *bought* earlier for a 'ton 'o money' too. Thomas is considering turning this guy over to Chim, as a Thank-You! And then maybe he won't kill me, like he killed Gwen ...)

"So, what's your story and make it quick. Decisions have to be made and I'm running out of time. So remember, don't jerk me around UNDERSTOOD!" Thomas grabs this guy by the collar and puts him against the wall. As if to say that he means business.

"Hey, that suits worth way over a thousand dollars that you're wrinkling and besides, I could probably snap you in two, so I might reconsider putting your hands on me, EVER again."

Thomas *gently lets go of him* and dusts his jacket off with his hand. He realizes that this guy could snap him into many pieces. Not that he's afraid to get in a 'scrape' if it calls for one. He's not one to back away from a fight, but he needs whatever information this

guy has. So, he's willing to listen, in the hope that it will help.
'So tell me your story ... Knight."
"Well, as you may know I own..."
"The Anvil2 Concrete company. I remember you, you supply concrete to many companies and agencies, including Transit."
"Boy, you really checked up on me."
"I'm waiting ... So why are they after you?"
"I tell you, the worst thing I ever did, was to buy a small printing company. All my troubles started from there."

"And next, your going to tell me about ZINIUM."

"Hey, who's telling this story—you OR me?"
"Go Ahead ...!"

He tells Thomas his story about acquiring the company because he collected on a bet. The company was going to go bankrupt, then he got awarded some contracts. One of them was to produce Collectible cards. He hired Max/Solutions and this guy Dorman suggested that they use this thing called Zinium.

Nothing new so far, Thomas thought to himself, as Jesse Knight continued. But you just never know ...
"Listen, we got to skip to the chase now! You said you had information about The Lone Rider. I need to know what that is NOW!" "Well the one thing I can tell you is" he continued ...

"THE LONE RIDER is ... *NOT* any *one* person!"

"What do you mean that he's not? How do you know?"
"Because I know the people who put it together, that's why, Special Agent Banner."

"It all stemmed from some lousy gambling debt by a Politician, as far as I know. And some other shady things that I'm not talking to you about, until I see my lawyer.

Politician. What Politician, Thomas thought to himself?

Chapter 41
The Fight

Museum

Thomas is reminded of what Dorland had said to him. That even he had to report to someone. Thomas decided to offer Knight protective custody and a phone call with his lawyer, if he went with him now. He knew he would be able to get more details tomorrow, but he had something to do tonight.

Jesse Knight agreed to go with him. When someone like that gives it up, then the situation absolutely has become—*very dangerous!*

Dorland's

Later that night, Thomas again kept vigil across from Dorland's apartment. He waited outside over two hours when he spotted Dorland walking out with a tall, younger man. He decided to follow him and they got into a cab and went to Midtown. They got out at a very trendy, relatively new restaurant called the Plates. The kind of place where people go to rub elbows with celebrities or to just be seen.

the Plates

He seemed to be very cozy with this man as they left the cab arm-in-arm. The place was packed, but they managed to get a table right by the window. Thomas crossed the street and hung out near a big potted plant that obscured them from seeing him, It did not however, prevent him from seeing them.

Then he saw something unusual, Dorland put his hand on the other man's leg. He then started to work his hand up this mans crouch. Later after dinner, they embraced each other and Dorland kissed this man hard on the lips. He walked with him outside and saw him into a cab and then hailed one for himself. Thomas followed him again and Dorland just headed home and into his building.

Dorland's

Thomas followed, then knocked on the door.

"Just a minute darling! I just knew you'd change your mind."
Dorland expected that it was his friend from the restaurant and said
   "Come on in, the doors open and I have a fabulous bottle of wine
for us to share, lover."

Thomas walked in and saw Matt Dorland sitting butt-naked on his
couch. There was some kind of gay porn on the TV and a look of
amusement on his face. Thomas couldn't help, but say to him ...
   "Hello Darling, I'm Back!"

   "I had no idea that you went that way Banner." There's a wide
smirk on his face. The one the cat makes in those "Alice' Books.

   "**I DON'T** and I most certainly didn't think you went that way
either, Dorland!" absolute disgust, registered on Dorland's face.
Thomas walked into the bathroom and grabbed a robe and threw it
right at Dorland's feet.
   "Here put this on. I want to get to the bottom of a few things ..."
   "Listen, I'm conformable in my own skin, I don't need a robe!"
   "Put it on now Dorland!"
   "Look, I've had a long evening and I'm really tired so, you can
talk to me at the office. Or if you want me to go to your office, just
tell me when and I'll have my lawyers meet me there." He yawns.
   "No. Sorry, I'm afraid were going to have to have this particular
conversation now, Matt. There's just no getting around it. In fact,
we should have had it weeks ago."

Dorland knew from his tone of voice and the fact that he called
him Matt that they *were* going to have this conversation now. He
stood up and put the robe on, but he tied it loosely.
   "First, did you have anything at all to do with the death of Gwen
Blissing?

   "No, I swear I didn't. I really liked Gwen and she was a bit of
a kink also. you just never were sure with her, which made it
exciting!"
Matt proceed to refill his glass of wine. "Would you like a glass
Banner? So what are doing here? You should be going after those
who were *responsible*, instead of wasting your precious time with
little old me."
   "Dorland, I'm being very serious now. I want to hear the whole
story and what your involvement is with 'The Lone Rider' and why

did you want to frame Arrondi?

[*Dorland moves over to the bar and sits on one of the stools. He pretends not to notice that his robe has opened slightly. Thomas sees his crotch. Thomas notices that he is, rather well hung.*]

That explains the attraction of Beatty Morgenstern to this slimeball. He can't believe she knows that he plays on BOTH teams?

"Cut that out Dorland and tie that robe tight. And, by the way, I'm the one asking the questions."

"I told you I have nothing more to say, now, goodnight Banner."

"Dorland you're going to talk ... even if I have to beat it out of you, you're gonna talk alright."

Thomas moves towards him in a very menacing way. Dorland decides that he's had enough of this guy, all in his face and since he's coming towards him rather fast, he decides to throw a karate front leg kick into Banner's side, to slow him down.

Banner is hit right below the ribs and crouches down from the impact. He puts up his hands now to protect himself from anything else he throws. They move around the room in a sort-of dance. Each one sizing up the other, looking for a way to take advantage.

Dorland takes a few more shots, of which Thomas is able to stop some. Others have landed and he is hurt. Thomas is getting beat and somehow he manages to maneuver himself over to the mantle. Dorland is about to make another move. Just then Thomas sees that vase he had picked up before in his apartment and hurls it really hard toward Dorland, he ducts and all you hear is ...
CRASH!

Dorland is so furious, that he decides to charge at him and finish the job. (He figures if he kills him, he can always claim, it was self-defense).

CRUNCH! Crumble!
Dorland catches Thomas with a karate chop to his upper torso. Thomas then grabs that same hand and whirls him around, until he lets go and Dorland crashes into his coffee table, breaking stuff. As Dorland goes to get up, Thomas catches him with a solid right-cross to the jaw and he indicates that he's had enough.

Chapter 42
The Pain!

Dorland's

Thomas feels like he's got a slightly broken rib on one side and his shoulder is so bruised that he can't lift his other arm up, at all.

He doesn't want to let on that he is that hurt. Thomas thinks to himself that he is lucky, the fight ended when it did, as he would have been too hurt to continue.

[Dorland is bleeding pretty good from his nose, his lip and he's got a deep cut above his left eye.]

Thomas is just about to continue to question him, when who should walk through the open door of Dorland's apartment, but *Mr. Chim and his associates!*

"How very fortunate it is for me, to meet up with the both of you in one place." He signals to his men "Search Banner and find the piece of paper I am looking for. Unfortunately trying to reason with you did not seem to be successful ...!" Thomas is grabbed by two of the men, while a manly looking woman named Sol, searches his wallet and pockets.

"We will talk again. at another time Mr. Chim, I will see you in the morning." He proceeded to try and head for the bedroom. Mr. Chim signals and one of the men hits Dorland hard in the gut!

He crumbles to the ground ...

"What the heck did you do that for? I thought we were partners. I thought our business was almost finished."
"Unfortunately for you Mr. Dorland, someone else is now in a position to deliver, what it is I seek."
"But we had a deal ..."
"Alas, we did. NOW WE DON'T!" Mr. Chim smashes his fist on the table.

"You have botched things up from the very beginning. From the people you chose to associate with, to the task right at hand and everything in between ..."

"But Mr. Chim, please, you must understand there are always circumstances that interfere with the best of plans."

"How dare you talk to me that way. What about circumstances? I'm a businessman, I understand this. But we haven't even begun to talk about costs! How much this enterprise has cost me so far?"

"I'm willing to take a smaller cut to help defray costs."
Dorland volunteers.

"Oh! that reminds me Banner, your ..."

"No need to go into details now." Thomas interrupts

"*Ah Ha!* I understand Mr. Banner, you're not interested in letting Dorland know that **Three Hundred Thousand Dollars** has been deposited in your bank account, for services rendered."

Dorland is totally surprised, caught off-guard with that revelation.

"Well, what do you know about that?" He smiles, shifts his body and turns and looks at Thomas.

"So you're one of us ... you've '*gone over to the dark side,*' is that how they phrase it?"
Mr. Chim signals to his man and he hits Dorland hard across the face. Dorland loses the smile ...

WHAM! Smash, Crunch!
He knocks over a few more Collectible Crystals. Dorland gets up ready to strike, when Chim's men grab him and hold him. They hold him really tight and he knows that something bad is about to happen to him. Then, Sol slowly walks over to him and takes out a blackjack and hits him several times across his body and face.
Wham! Bang! THUD!

Dorland's body slumps to the floor. Sol goes into the kitchen and gets some water and a small towel. She then proceeds to treat his wounds, wiping and blotting them very gently. As he comes to, he goes to wipe his lip and looks up at her. Right then she says ...

"I know you liked that Matt! do you want me to do some more?
Did it hurt enough OR should I be rougher?!"

Wait a minute! Thomas thinks to himself, somethings not right here. It's like this performance was put on for my benefit ... like maybe they already know each other. Thomas says. "Nice Show!"

"You are a smart man Banner. I would've guessed that you already had figured out that none of this was real (in a sense). That this was done just for my amusement." Mr. Chim continues "Matt, Sol —you were really excellent, what a performance! **BRAVO!**"

"However Banner, *you will not be as fortunate ...* "

Just then the Calvary shows up, in the form of that BASTARD Slinger, *who I was never so glad to see in my entire life*, Thomas thinks to himself. And the best part is that he walked in and has the drop on them. He has his service revolver and his second gun both drawn and turned on all of them. Thomas is very grateful ...

"All of you get your hands up and move over there by the mantle. Dorland, that means you too! Banner, get over here by me."

"Why'd you come in here with your guns drawn?" Thomas asked. "I saw somethings I didn't like ... Looked like the good guy was losing, which is not good. And, they are definitely the bad guys!" Slinger underscores this, by pointing to them.

"I don't understand, *I thought, you're one of the bad guys ...?*"

"NOPE! *I've been working undercover!* I've been after these guys all along." Slinger continues looking at all those with their hands up. "Ladies and gentlemen, in a moment or two some uniformed officers are going to be here to read you your rights, but I might as well tell you that you are all under arrest." There's a big grin on his face now!

Officers arrive on the scene and the building is surrounded and there's a small heavily armed tactical force with them.

Mr. Chim screams ...

"DON'T JUST STAND THERE, DO SOMETHING!"

One of his men pulls out a knife and is shot in the shoulder, two others attempt to get their guns out, but realize there is no hope and surrender.

Just then, Mr. Chim and Sol run into one of the bedrooms and barricade the door. She stands guard right at the door and fires several shots through it. Luckily no one in the other room is hit by the shots. Chim tries to make good his escape ...

"That's it Sol, keep them pinned down."

He opens a window and climbs outside and stands on the ledge.

He thinks he can move across to the next apartment or try to climb up to the roof. The roof seems safer.

WHAM!

The tactical guys break down the door and even though Sol keeps firing, she is bowled over by them, as she empties her weapon. She is disarmed and the cuffs are slapped on her, but she has bought enough time for Chim to make good on his escape, to the roof!

Meanwhile, Banner goes into the hall and up the stairs to the roof. He searches for Chim going slowly, with his gun drawn.

It's amazing what goes through your mind during moments like this, he thinks. I'm just days away from retirement and I managed to survive everything in my career so far that has happened to me and now once again, I face my mortality.

Several of those tactical officers enter the roof, Thomas turns to look at who's coming behind him. Just then Chim *fires his gun ...!*

BAM! BAM!

Thomas is *hit!* He turns and fires and hits Chim in the leg, Chim hobbles away and one of the tactical officers shoots him in his other leg. He goes down and says ...

"That's enough, I surrender ... I give up—*don't shoot!*" He throws his gun out. The officers throw the cuffs on him and take him away.

Slinger comes up and asks ...

"Is everythings OK? Better let the medics take a look at that shoulder. Looks like you're lucky, the bullet went right through you. You should live!"

"Thanks for that vote of confidence."

"After they check you out and bandage you. Banner, you and I need to go for a long, tall drink ... maybe even a few of them."

"I think I'd like that and I'm buying." Thomas replies.

"Before they took him away, Dorland said something about the fact that you have a 'Couple of Hundred Grand' now, so I guess you can afford to buy—come on lets go in my car and start to celebrate your good fortune. As a matter-of-fact, I think we should go to Milt's. If that's OK with you, Banner."

"That will do nicely Slinger."

Chapter 43
The Discovery!

Milt's

Back at the bar, Slinger and Banner order a round of drinks, the two continue the small talk they started in the car.

"Alright Slinger, start at the beginning and tell me how you got all wound up in all this? Oh! and try to explain. if you were on our side. Why did you shoot at me over at Anvil2?!"

"*I shot into the sky*, if I wanted to hit you Banner, it would not really have been a problem, as I'm considered an *expert marksman.*" He looks at me and laughs. I want to believe him, but I'm just not sure? Thomas wonders if Slinger is really OK!

"Anyhow, a long time ago my boss, Inspector Jawatson asked me to go undercover on a case he wanted worked on, involving Transit and this fellow Dorland. Seems Mayor Betrand wanted something done about corruption there. He wanted to get tough and expose a number of things that up until that moment, were never tied together neatly. It seemed that up 'til now, Transit had always received nothing more than a slap on the wrist, at best.

So, the investigation goes underway and my 'cover' is that I'm a loose cannon and corruptible myself. I was then planted at ClubWINK and worked as a gun for hire, in terms of security. The dirtier I appeared to be, the closer I got to those I wanted to nail. *—And I wanted to nail all of them!"*

Another investigation was ongoing—about illegalities along the Waterfront and yet another on price-gouging in the City. Slinger explained that the Mayor wanted this to be an example of how tough his administration was going to be on corruption and crime.

"Betrand, wanted to be known, as the nations CRIMEBUSTER!"

"Waitress bring us another round, one for me and one for my

friend Thomas Banner ... My RICH friend, Thomas Banner. So how did you wind up with so much money again Thomas?"

"Nevermind that for now." Thomas still hasn't decided if he is going to keep the money or not. Please continue the story.

Slinger goes on. "Well, I guess you know that Dorland is up to his eyeballs in it. And Mr. Chim, owned a holding company called ChimEXP, the original company that sold those computers that were crap, to Transit. The ones that 'Lorraine' Beatty Morgenstern was told to approve, by circumventing the Bidding process."

He explained that "Dorland had a real strangle hold on her and he was involved in a lot of 'sick shit' in his personal life. He was bisexual and kinky and into hard core S&M and he hurt or caused a number of people to be hurt, both physically and mentally.

He was looking to have James Arrondi—one of my inside sources killed, so I had to prevent that. Some Buffs that he knew had a story that had already been concocted, about a letter to be signed by the Buff Brigade. I figured it would work better, if it was signed 'THE LONE RIDER' This character was created to take the heat off Dorland himself and some of the others. So we put the story out there. Every time I was close to nailing these bastards, YOU would totally wind up getting in the way. Of course you had no way of knowing what was going on ... and luckily, Mel Oats, the Editor of The Daily Flush, was in on it too. They even put out that bogus reward money that no one will be able to claim 'cause ...

"THERE IS NO LONE RIDER!!!"

Thomas looks at him in total disbelief. "You mean to tell me that I was nothing more than—just a patsy, in this little scheme of yours. That my partner, JOSEPH SORELO and all those others —HAD DIED IN VAIN!??? Why I ought to ..."

"Look I know hearing this isn't easy, but if you were in on it at anytime, the whole thing would have blown up and two plus years of undercover work and coordination would have been shot. Besides, it's bad enough, that I just had to blow my cover tonight.
It would have been better if I lasted until the deadline had passed.

If you don't believe me, you can check with Jawatson or Oates or PETERS or Betrand for that matter. Check out what I've been telling you about, and see if they don't all agree, that *they were most definitely in on it.*"

Thomas is jut so sick to his stomach. He can't believe, the level of betrayal that has occurred. especially from Peters!
He worked with him for all these years and he couldn't be trusted, to be informed about what was going on. **Holy Shit!**

He thinks about the incredible price this case has cost him. *His marriage, his partner, his morals, his vows—**HIS SOUL and his MIND!*** How could he continue on ... Still, he was fascinated by the story and *he hated himself* most of all, because of that.

Slinger continued, "here are some other things that you don't know. By the way, I had been trailing Rimsum for a couple of weeks and I couldn't BELIEVE IT when, of ALL the people in the world, he had to slam into YOUR car." Slinger knew he had Thomas' attention.
    "By the way, Ronald Rimsum and those three others that were killed. You didn't find any money, drugs or weapons there. Why? Because they had already been taken, by those who had killed them." Thomas says "Please go on, this is fascinating." *It's as if he's in a bad dream and doesn't know how to wake himself up.*

"What you also didn't know, was that Ronald Rimsum had just gone in the house from the back, moments before you knocked and identified yourself. He thought that you might be the killers, but for some reason, he opened the door and then panicked and ran. Who could blame him, after all he had stumbled upon, all that blood ... EVERYWHERE ...!"
    All of them in the house were killed by Mr. Chim's associates. That sick one called Sol, really enjoyed torturing and then killing Rimsum. I hear, she may have even let Dorland *watch!!!*"

Funny, Thomas thought, all this time, he was sure that Slinger had, had something to do ... with the murders!

"*Thomas, you really made everything harder for me.* Every time you got close to the truth, I had to do something or send someone

174

your way, to take you off the trail. If you think about it, every time you found an avenue of discovery, suddenly you'd be thrust in another direction.

In fact, *I was starting to run out of false leads to throw you.*" Slinger continued watching Banner react almost as if he was mesmerized. He said to him that "Thomas you should have another drink." In fact, he told the waitress, "to *leave the bottle* now!" Dorland was just getting warmed up.

"I guess you're feeling pretty sorry for yourself by now Thomas. But what about me? I had to live that life. Hang out in every gutter and shit-hole you could ever imagine. I've done and seen things that no one should EVER have to do, or see ... or say!"

Thomas, was starting to get buzzed and was now adrift in a sea of DISCOVERY! Slinger continued on, even though Thomas really didn't want to hear it. It was so painful.

"I'm the one that sent over all those guys *making-up shit* about the job at Transit. I told them to really lay it on *extra thick*! Most of them were ex-cons or my snitches, some were truly disgruntled workers, but *with an axe to grind*. I mingled them in so well, that you probably couldn't make head nor tails of any it. I radomly picked the date on that letter from The Lone Rider. I had the equipment that it was typed on etc. So many false leads, so much *Bullshit!* None of those dates and/or times anyone provided were REAL! *Pretty neat piece of work ...*
—right Banner?"

It was as if he was just setting him up for the kill, at least that's what Thomas was thinking. Slinger was holding a couple more Aces in his hand it seemed and he was just about to play them.

One at a time. Slowly—he would play them ...

Chapter 44
The Horror...

Milt's

Now, Slinger is talking, as if he is about to unfurl, his great masterpiece!

"Then, I go to work setting up Beatty Morgenstern."

Slinger continues and Thomas between the liquor and the subject matter is totally absorbed (as best he can) considering he is starting to feel the effects of all the liquor, he's been drinking here.

"I know her relationship with Dorland is really bizarre! I figured I could use that to my advantage. And, I also had someone on the *inside*. Gail Diaz!"

Thomas has been so blind that he's sure that as soon as Slinger lays it out for him, that it should have been obvious from the very beginning, he even had Diaz, for crying out loud ... "Go Ahead!" he shouts!

"Diaz had written some bad checks, back in the day. I discovered that fact quite by accident, but I knew I could use it, as leverage to ensure that she would cooperate, when the time came. I knew that Beatty was under a lot of pressure. She was going to crack maybe, but not soon enough, so I gave her a little push.

I knew she was probably afraid of Dorland and Mr. Chim etc., but not enough to come to me yet and spill her guts. A very tough woman with a heart of gold, she had a full past and an interesting to say the least present, and a tremendous number of possible futures. Anyhow ...

"It was me who had sent that personal letter from ...
'THE LONE RIDER' and had it delivered to her office."

Slinger continues to tell his tale. Stopping every now and then to have another sip of his drink.

"Since Dorland was a total RICH A-hole, I figured that she might turn to Diaz, as a way of alleviating herself of that awful burden she had been keeping ... Diaz would guide her to me and I would have the piece of the puzzle that could bring down the whole house of cards ..."

"As my luck would have it, thats exactly what SHOULD have happened. *But it didn't, did it Banner?*" he said.

"But it didn't, because your partner Joseph managed to get himself *killed!* Beatty was just about plum scared out of her wits because he had been working on THE LONE RIDER case. She reasoned that if he could be killed that easy, then for sure, she would be killed on September 17, 2011!
No matter what Gail did, she couldn't get Beatty to go and see me and spill her guts. So I had to devise another way to get her to open up. By talking to you and hoping that you would keep Gail in the loop ...!"

Slinger was a little more animated now. Maybe it was the liquor, maybe it was just part of reliving it all again. Every man has his demons.

"Oh! I almost forgot something. I was going to plant some bugs in your vehicles to keep an eye on you and see that you didn't interfere in my plans. And lo and behold, your friend Christopher goes and does it for me...TERRIFIC! Since I already had bugged his office, I knew exactly what was happening to you on most occasions." I'm really sorry about Chris though, I had no idea that DeFontaine was going to shoot and KILL him. Anyhow, here's the rest of it ...

"The one thing that I didn't foresee was that you, you poor schmuck, would fall for Beatty! *Like everybody else on the planet!!!*" Slinger felt real sorry for Banner now.

"You were really starting to get close to the answers in your investigation and you caught her at a time when she was most vulnerable ... I had to step in and pull that prank at the Hotel. I needed to break you two up and I figured that, that would probably do the trick."

Thomas felt as if he was nothing more than a puppet, whose mere

177

strings were being pulled, absolutely at will. It was a surreal experience listening to Slingers explanations.

"Fast forward to tonight. I had to go and BLOW MY COVER after over two years of an investigation, because of *you!* I had to go and *Save Your Ass!* When I had a good mind to have them go and beat you to a pulp." **Man, I was so pissed at you ...!!!!**

Now, normally if anyone ever had talked to Thomas, the way that Slinger had talked to him tonight, He would have torn him or her to pieces. But he was so drained, so tired ... so spent, that at this point, he just had to sit there and take it.

Like he had given it to others in the past. Now, he knew what it was like, to be on the receiving end.

Chapter 45
The Ring...

Milt's

"So you're probably wondering what this whole thing was really about?" Slinger is now reading entries from a note pad he brought with him, from the glove compartment of his car.

Slinger held up his hands and counts on the fingers of one, then the other, while he says out loud ...

"Several counts of:
Murder, Kidnapping, Bribery, Theft, Torture, Prostitution, Car Theft, Forgery, Obscenity, Collusion, Obstruction, Malfeasants, Intimidation, Money Laundering, Interstate Theft, Corruption of Officials, Mismanagement of Funds, Fraudulent Contracts and at least another dozen or maybe two charges thrown in, just for good measure." Slinger knows he has prevailed.

"This 'Ring' as you refered to them, was responsible for a total of at least twelve murders, both here and abroad. They managed to abscond with almost eighteen million dollars skimmed off the top. And they have killed at least 16 people, that we know of"

"They have created wholesale havoc, unleashed a wrath upon people that has resulted in at least four maimings and almost one hundred and fifty two civilians and twenty-two law enforcement officers hospitalized Worldwide. And as a direct result of their involvement, there are several structures that may or may not be on the verge of collapse."

He continues, "with any luck, their high-priced lawyers will have some of them back on the streets in a week or less, but more than likely, the major players like Chim and Dorland will receive stiff sentences. Although Dorland, with his kind of family money and connections, may just get-off Scott-Free.
So much for that end of the justice system ..."

"So, the evidence that was gathered will be given to a Federal prosecutor, who will attempt to have the book thrown at them all Thomas. Of course, even though we will try to connect all of them to this Ring, they will all probably have to be tried separately, for us to get any convictions. And, since some of the contracts that they rigged, pertained to State and City agencies and used Federal monies, the charges should stick."

Slinger looks at the time and realizes that they have talked through the night, it is just about Sunrise!

"You know what really irks me Thomas?"
"What's that Slinger?"
"I was **thisclose** to actually finding out where that Collectible ClickCard was. You know, the one that so many people had died for. " Slinger was about to call it a night ...
"Maybe, I can get one of them to confess, as to where it is?"

"Before you go, I need to know, who was it driving the car that almost killed my family and myself and the thing that haunts me the most ..." Thomas took a really long deep breath, then said:

"Why?...Why did my partner have to die, Slinger?"

"Oh yeah ... the Allcus thing."
What the heck is that?"
"Both brothers were in this thing up to their eyeballs too. The thing is that they were both approaching it from slightly different angles. Slinger pauses for a moment, the drinking having finally taken a toll on him. He has to concentrate, to make sure he remembers it all. Now where to start ...

"Remember when we first met and you wanted to look at one of the Allcus' apartments and I clued you into the fact that there were actually two apartments.
Well, since we had gotten there first ... I did some snooping around and discovered something like a 'journal'—A book with some notes and other pages stuffed in it." (He pulls out of his jacket a small copy he made of it.)
"Later, when I got a chance to read it, it turned out that he had been after the Collectible Card too. Your partner got killed because Carlos Allcus had some kind of insane jealousy concerning

Scanner Simmons.
Anyway later on, he was killed by one of Mr. Chim's thugs.
It was such a real inept attempt to make it look so much, like it was
a suicide—*which it wasn't.*"
Slinger mentions the fact that after further investigation, that it was
determined, that it was in fact, a *murder!*

By the way Slinger says "Nice job on spotting that stuff on the
paintings in the Allcus apartments. If you're wondering how
I know that, Jesse Knight told me. Somehow, we missed that."

"As for the other brother, Winston, he had also been looking to
acquire the ClickCard, but he had been doing it through a known
associate of Mr. Chim's, Max Dorland. Since Winston was a Buff,
he was the prefect person to add to the search. So at some point
both brothers were enticed to join the ring, the lure being the
Collectible ClickCard.

No one would have suspected either one of them until, a large
amount of cash and two checks, one a piece from each brother
turned up in Ronald Rimsum coat. I guess she missed that small
inside pocket, when Sol searched him, then tortured him? "

Slinger turns to Thomas and grabs his arm and helps him up. It was
time to go home or to work, for both of them.

"As to your original question, I don't really know who tried to
kill you guys (or at least scare you to death). My guess is that it
was Dorland? He was just trying to intimidate you by to sending
you a message ...! Anyway, you probably thought that it was
someone else."

"I thought it was Carlos Allcus ..."

Chapter 46
The Finish

Milt's

Slinger winds up his long story by saying. "I discovered that there was a lot more involved in this Murder at Transit case. Much broader implications, than what was in, the original scope of the investigation. More that Jawatson even realized. There was an international crime 'Ring' involved and a plethora of other players, including corrupt Transit management people, consultants and Federal, State and local Politicians involved. Some stuff was way out of our jurisdiction or yours. That part of the case went directly to the Justice Department, and was passed on up, but our through investigation formed the core." And then he says ...

"*Luckily for you*, the majority of the evidence had been gathered on the Federal and State level. As for me, I got most of what I came for. Some minor stuff didn't quite get tied up, but in the end I think the job got done."

Slinger looks at him and says...

"Thomas, about that money thing ... I'm just going to pretend that I didn't hear anything about it yet. I'm sure that in the end, you'll do the right thing. But whatever you do, you had better do it rather *quickly!* Because I'm sure that someone has, or will spill their guts, to one of those Detectives back at headquarters.

"One last thing I want you to think about Thomas Banner ... I've been asked to work at the Federal level now. Some real high-profile stuff. I think we could team-up and work together and really make an impact. The choice my friend, is yours...

Slinger reaches out his hand to Thomas, to shake it. Thomas just turns away and starts walking in a different direction. He goes off towards the sunrise ...

Banner thinks, me work with him? "Yeah, that'll be the day ..."

Chapter 47
The Ghosts!

The City

Thomas really wanted to hate Slinger, but he just couldn't. He couldn't forget that he probably saved Thomas' life. But shake his hand—*he just couldn't do that either ...*

He was just numb, between the weather, the alcohol and the fact that his guts had just been KICKED-IN *several times!*

He was going to walk down to the river, because that was the one place he might be able to find solace. At this moment, he was truly, one of the 'lost souls,' on this planet.

It wasn't too long a walk and as he moved through the hustle and bustle of this Metropolis, he kept running through his head, all of the things that Slinger had said. They haunted him, they plagued him ... they tortured him, they tortured his soul.

Maybe it was the cold air, maybe it was that inner core of his, that allowed him to 'snap back into it' Suddenly his head was clear. He knew what he had to do and why he would do it.

"Escape!" he shouted out loud, as he climbed over the handrail overlooking the water and said "Luckily I have that small life insurance policy that should provide for my wife Christine and my sons. This will not be a hard decision."

"I have no career."
"And, I have no dignity left ..."
"I have no life left EITHER."

Just then, a strange thing happened. He understands now that while this would not be a *hard* decision to make—*it would NOT be the right one for him.* He determined that he deserved *better than this!* He was going to turn his life around. After all, this obsession with THE LONE RIDER case was over.

In the end, it really didn't really matter. He was free now to make whatever choice he choose.

—Even Slinger's offer ...?

What really did matter, was that he had finally gotten to let go, of the 'GHOST' of his dead partner.
The GHOST of his dead marriage.
The GHOST of his career.
The GHOST of his inability to learn to relax in life.

The GHOST of always being told by someone, what to do and what NOT to do...

He was finally free. Really FREE, for the first time in his life.

He was free of the GHOSTS of the bad things he had done in life.

And that he had learned to 'EMBRACE the GHOST' of his dead friend Christopher Drake. Who toiled everyday down in the depths. In the belly of the beast, but out of everyone he knew, he was the only one who had known, how to really *LIVE!*

He also knew that he would never be free of the GHOSTS of the DEAD!

They would continue to haunt him, but in a totally different way then you would think. 'They' would continue to haunt him now, to really LIVE! That he should live for those in life, who no longer could.

That, he should live life to the fullest, with no regrets!

He knew that he did not have a tremendous number of years left. But, *live his life, he fully intended to ...*

*Of course, now that offer from Slinger would haunt him, but he promised himself that he would try **not** to think about it, at all ...*

Chapter 48
The Plan

Waterfront

Thomas climbs back over the fence and takes his cell-phone out of his pocket and calls Jersey, Joseph's old girlfriend, again ...

[Right after Gwen was killed outside the bank, he had called Jersey to do him a favor. They had kept in touch and would see each other on occasion, after the death of Joseph, to try to comfort each other. That friendship got to be extremely close. A romance of sorts.

Anyway, He asked Jersey to go to the bank and go see a friend of his, and his favorite bank Vice-President, Brenda Craig (also by chance, Dorland's too). Jersey was instructed to pick up a manilla envelope for him, from her.

After she got out of the bank, she was instructed to go to hail a cab and go directly to the Airport, and to wait for Thomas. If he didn't show up by noon, she was to go home, open the envelope and know that he was grateful for everything they had shared together.]

TaskForce HQ

Banner did not show up for work today. He was missed and several calls had come in looking for him. they included one from his wife. Peters made several phone calls and inquires as to where he might be. He dispatched a unit to check all of his usual haunts, to see if he was Ok!

[Peters eventually had gotten a phone call from Slinger bringing him up to speed as to what had happen between Banner and himself. He assured Peters that Banner was strong enough to handle it and that there was no cause for concern. His papers were in, in days he would be officially retired with a decent pension and a nice wife and family. He probably just needed to be left alone ...

Slinger never mentioned the money and neither did Peters. He assumed that by now, he must know something about it.]

185

The really big news, that was all over the papers, TV, Cable and the Internet, was the big bust that had happened last night. Peters was happy that his department (per his agreement prior, with Jawatson and Slinger) was partially responsible and given partial credit for bringing down, this international band of cutthroats!

The City could rest at ease, now that there was no longer a threat to Transit. In fact, Mayor Betrand was going to have a big press conference in just a couple of hours, to announce formally to the Public that there was no longer any cause for concern about THE LONE RIDER'...!

His City was going to be safer than ever, due to the diligence of his administration, and of course as a consequence—Him!

Airport

Jersey was getting nervous, she followed Thomas' instructions to the letter and hoped that he would show up on time.

In the meantime, she had spent most of her time watching the big bust of the 'Ring' on the TV there. She was amazed at the coverage and the depth of the investigation. She saw that Peters, The Mayor and this Detective Slinger were all there. Thomas should have been too. But she was glad, he chose to go away with her instead.

She hoped that he was alright, but she hadn't heard anything from him and worried that he hadn't done anything foolish.

And what of Thomas?

Well, you know how sometimes in the back of most peoples brains there's something that allows you to think about and plan the demise of a coworker, or to perhaps, to runaway on the back of a motorcycle or do something outrageous like come in with that full color tattoo of Aunt Ethel on your shoulder, that you promised yourself that you would do someday.

Or you'd sit and daydream about what you would do if you hit the really big multi-state lottery.

On several occasions, over many years (especially when he was drinking) Thomas had planned in his mind the perfect murder, the perfect robbery and *THE PERFECT ESCAPE!*

Over and over he had planned all of these and so precisely, down to the minute— *how to do them all separately, or together!*

Thomas thought it was important that he have a great back-up plan, just in case something had gone wrong, with his very ordinary life. *And, this was it ...*

Before he grabbed a cab and headed out to the Airport. He walked over to a park that he had always visited and behind the bathroom building, in the dirt he had buried (when no one was watching) a small portfolio case, wrapped in plastic. He retrieved said case and he didn't even care, whether anyone saw him do it or not. He then hailed a cab.

Next, He made a stop at a men's store in the City on the way and changed in the cab into a casual shirt and jeans, and sneakers.

Thomas then opened the case in the cab and made sure that the contents had not changed. Inside were two new passports with their pictures, with fake names. (Believe it or not, Jersey knew someone who could supply them—for a couple of thousand dollars) A couple of blank checks and some other identifying papers, using their new names. Their *brand new names* were Frank Nits, and Michele Nits. Their cover story is that they are newlyweds, off on their honeymoon!

Meanwhile Jersey went and bought a magazine to try and take her mind off of the envelope. As she is walking back to her seat, a Security Guard walks directly up to her and says ...

"Excuse me Miss."
Jersey freaks out, but tries to remain cool, and replies...
"What do you want?"
"I'm sorry to disturb you Miss. I just wanted to alert you to the fact that when you recently made a purchase, you left and you, didn't close your purse. I just wouldn't want someone to take advantage of the situation."
"Why thank you sir."
"Glad to be of service Miss. Have a safe flight."

WHOA! she thought, that was it ... BUSTED!

With that, she holds on even tighter to that manilla envelope, but turns and sees Thomas and says loud enough, for the Guard to hear.
"Oh! Hello darling! I've missed you so."

Thomas motions to her and whispers into her ear, as they turn and walk away.
"Tell me, Did you have some kind of problems with Security?"
"No, Everything is all right. Lets go get our tickets. By the way, where are we going Thomas?"
"Well, you get to pick my dear."
"Then I think that we should go to Patrine, off the Coast of Berlitz for the Winter and Razzerstan for the Summer."

They pick up their tickets and head to the gate area. They have about 15 or 20 minutes before their flight takes off. Thomas and Jersey sit and hold hands, while they watch TV.
Thomas is sitting, watching the 'exclusive story' of the capture of the mastermind, of the 'Ring,' responsible for dozens of murders and millions stolen. Poor, shy Mr. Chim, is now a *celebrity!*

Thomas thinks to himself that he can't believe he's about to leave the country with a beautiful women, that is not his wife. Jersey isn't Christine or Beatty for that matter, but what a *consolation prize ... !!!*

So, he's going to be considered a fugitive and can never go home. So What? Who cares? Three Hundred Grand buys a lot of so what? who cares? He figures Jersey and him will buy a tiny little villa, somewhere near the water and live out the rest of their days. He sits there and just gets lost in the fantasy of it all ...

Meanwhile, Jersey is lost in her own fantasy. Thomas is a nice enough guy, but he's no Joseph. So she figures. she'll go with him as this will take her, out of her misery, temporarily.

And then, depending on where they go and the circumstances, she'll spend the rest of her time *plotting his murder!*

After all, Three Hundred Grand and a still *'smokin' hot'* face and body should find her *plenty of 'volunteers'* to do the dirty deed.

If Thomas only knew, but she's sure, he doesn't *suspect* a thing!

Chapter 49
The Plane

Airport

A couple of more minutes and they will start to board the plane.

Thomas won't be missed just yet. They'll figure that he's busy sulking 'cause his pride is hurt and that eventually he will come in and officially retire. *But by then, it will be too late!*

Just then, On TV, in the background, from some file footage from —a scene at police headquarters. Just for a moment, he thought he saw someone, who he never got to meet. He only knows about him from his picture, in one of his files. He's pretty sure that he saw a 6 foot 6 inch guy that weighted almost 300 hundred pounds. A guy named Lou Long. But nah ... it couldn't be ... could it?

Thomas asked himself, what would a guy whose supposed to be a loon, be doing at police headquarters anyway? And then he remembered something that Gwen had said about Lou:

"Anyhow, he was a very sharp guy, who on occasion would come in, and pretend, that he was out of his mind—just for the FUN of it!" That was the quote.

Is it possible that it was him? And if it is, then ... **BINGO!**

If that WAS him, then I'm pretty sure that I probably do know *where* that Collectible ClickCard is. Thomas figures this is going to be easy money. He'll leave the country now and *come back in awhile*, when the heat dies down and his tan is better. **And get his hands on that card ...**

Thomas and Jersey board their airplane and kickback in there luxurious 1st class seats, with drinks in hand and *not a care in the World!*

AND ALL THAT MONEY ...

Chapter 50
The Conclusion

Airplane

Jersey fell asleep, almost as soon as they took off from the Airport.
It was to be a somewhat long flight, so Thomas thought he'd have
time to sleep later. And then he realizes ...

WOW! **Tomorrow is SEPTEMBER 17, 2011!**

Thomas figures to be in a whole 'nother country by then. About as
far away from the investigation into who was 'The Lone Rider'
case, as he could possibly be. Still, he can't stop thinking about it.

On one hand, it seems that the only real 'concrete' proof that
a **'Murder at Transit'** is going to be committed ...
—is to the Public!

*"It may not be tomorrow, but it will come eventually, because of
what they did to that place and nobody had the courage to say
STOP! —Somebody needs to come forward ..."*

This, according to what some of those disgruntled workers had said
to him, during his investigation of the case. *"I think they're wrong!
And I think there's always hope!"* Thomas says in a whisper.

On the other hand, something about this case, still doesn't fit
right. Based on everything he knows and everything that Slinger
told him, something doesn't make sense, something is missing.
He's just got to make, all the pieces fit. But he still has a hunch,
that there will be—a murder committed tomorrow, a ...

... MURDER AT TRANSIT! by **THE LONE RIDER!**

If it happens, Thomas' sure he knows, WHO's going to do it!!!

THE END

About the author

CLIF MILITELLO
is an Art Director,
Cartoonist and Caricaturist,
living in Astoria, Queens NY

Back in 1989, Clif created
2500 spot illustrations for
The Official Pictionary ® Dictionary
which was published by Perigee Books,
a part of The Putnam Publishing Group

NOTES

NOTES

NOTES

NOTES

Dedication

This book is dedicated to the following people, who I hold dear.

KRISTINE
Diane, Donna & James,
Tom, Diane, Christopher and Michele,
Sadie & Paul, Brenda & Craig, Carole & Richie,
Helen & Ralph, Lorraine & Beardsley,
Bill & Joanne, Kurt & Mary Lynn,
And, Various Family Members, too numerous to mention.

My friends:
Rick Catania,
Chim, Gary, Moti, Bill, Carole, Krissy, Isabella, Tom, Anne, Mel,
And to those others I worked with, for almost twenty-five years.
You know who you are ... Thank You!

Winston, George, Gail, Rosemary, Diane, Clinton, Charles, Charlie,
Roger, Larry and the Friday Crew.

My QV guys:
1st Group: Bob S, Cliff S, Richie M, Chris P, Jerry P
2nd Group: Joe, Pete, Bob, Arnie, John,

A tip of the hat to:
Carmen
'Brother' Ron
Gerald D, Patty S,
Archit, Chuck, Tommy McD,
Joanne, Lucille, Sol, Suzy, Laura, Dru, Lynn, Denise, Rita, Heather,
TEAM MILITELLO

People, who have made a tremendous difference, in my life:
Lorraine Graham/culture
Warren Eisenberg/computers
Ira Russack/business
Hans Hammerquist/ingenuity
PA Tippet/opportunity
Tom Militello/everything else

Places/Companies that impacted my life: New York City, Astoria,
Queensview, Long Island, Hospital for Special Surgery, Fresh Air Fund,
La Salle Academy, Canal Jeans, Sam Flax and MTA NYC Transit and

The 'MAC,' of course!